PANORAMIC CHINA

PANORAMIC CHINA

China's Sports
Honors and Dreams

FOREIGN LANGUAGES PRESS

First Edition 2008

ISBN 978-7-119-05390-5
© Foreign Languages Press, Beijing, China, 2008
Published by Foreign Languages Press
24 Baiwanzhuang Road, Beijing 100037, China
http: //www.flp.com.cn

Distributed by China International Book Trading Corporation
35 Chegongzhuang Xilu, Beijing 100044, China
P.O.Box 399, Beijing, China

Printed in the People's Republic of China

Foreword

In the eight decades since the 1920s, the Chinese people have made three great achievements under the leadership of the Chinese Communist Party. The first was the revolution. After more than 20 years of indomitable fighting and resistance, finally in 1949 the People's Republic of China was founded to represent the basic interests of the Chinese people. The Chinese nation had finally won total independence and a new China full of vitality arose in the eastern part of the world. The second great achievement was rebuilding. What the old political power structure had left behind was chaos, poverty, weakness, and damages. Exerting huge efforts, the newborn China restored the national economy within a very short period of time, and gradually stabilized and improved the social life of its citizens. Next, building on an extremely poor foundation, China carried out planned development of industry, agriculture and other sectors, establishing an independent and fairly complete industrial system and a national economic system. The third achievement was development. From the late 1970s and early 1980s on, China firmly stepped onto the road of reform and opening-up to the outside world, pressing ahead with reforms starting from agriculture and gradually moving toward industry and other sectors, and continuing the process of opening up which had originated from the coastal areas toward the inland regions. More than 20 years have passed, and China has witnessed an earth-shattering transformation. Her national economy has maintained development at a fast pace. Dramatic developments have occurred in both China's overall national strength and the standard of living of her citizens. All this has opened up broad prospects for the building of a prosperous society and the realization of modernization in China.

Deng Xiaoping, one of the greatest men of our times, once said that "development is the utmost truth." In China today, every domain and every profession are continuing the implementation of the "utmost truth" as defined by Deng Xiaoping to foster further development of the nation. Through practice and experimentation over several dozens of years, China has realized that development must follow the principles of being scientific, sustainable and harmonious. Not only must development aim to continuously raise the people's standard of living, but it must also benefit our descendants and not cause disastrous consequences for our Earth while trying to better the livelihood of humanity. Not only must China succeed with these developments for herself, but she must also work with all the countries of the world for mutual benefit, developing together and building a harmonious society and a peaceful international environment. Based upon the outlook of scientific and harmonious development, China is striving to make this "Third Great Achievement."

The series on "Panoramic China" consist of two sections. The first section, which has been published, focuses on introducing provinces, cities, and autonomous regions of China over an extended period of time. The second section, which is currently being published, tells about the work of different sectors, departments, and trades of China in order to introduce the practices and concepts of various aspects of development, the accomplishment of the "Third Great Achievement," as well as the challenges and opportunities China faces today. These introductions are realistic with factual descriptions and colorful pictures. It is our sincere hope that by reading this set of books, our readers will learn more about the plan, the work and the achievements of certain sectors, departments or trades and also their efforts and experiences in the peaceful development of the country. In particular, readers will see how, step by step, the Chinese people from different walks of life are turning their dreams for development, happiness and peace into reality.

The Chinese women's volleyball players cheering after their victory

ATHENS 2004

Liu Xiang races at the Athens Olympics.

The Chinese badminton team defended its title at the Thomas Cup finals in 2006 and captured the trophy for the sixth time. The picture shows the players cheering after their success.

Shen Xue and Zhao Hongbo captured the bronze medal twice in the pairs competition in figure skating at the 19th and 20th Olympic Winter Games.

Yao Ming and his teammates celebrating their victory that placed the Chinese team among the best eight at the 2004 Olympic Games in Athens

Dragon Boat Race, a traditional sport in China with a history of over a thousand years

Contents

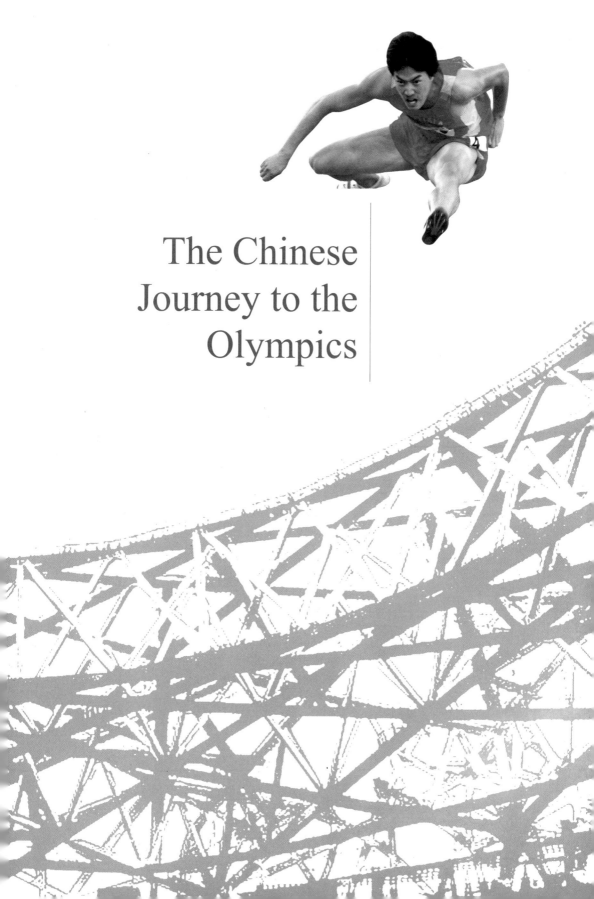

The Chinese Journey to the Olympics

China and the Olympics before 1984 |

The Chinese women's volleyball players hugging each other after taking the gold medal at the 1984 Olympic Games in Los Angeles

China put an end to its "zero" gold medal record at the 23rd Olympic Games in Los Angeles in the United States in 1984 by taking 15 gold medals, 8 silver medals and 9 bronze medals. This initiated a new era in Chinese Olympic history. Since then, Chinese athletes have kept winning Olympic medals and breaking world records on the same occasions.

It can be said that the year 1984 was a significant watershed so far as China's participation in the Olympic Games is concerned. For most Chinese, their memory of the Olympics begins with that year. However, if we turn back the pages of Olympic history, we discover that China's relationship with the Olympic Games began far earlier. It went on intermittently like a hidden current flowing in the long river of Olympic history, sometimes visible and sometimes invisible.

■The earliest connection between China and the Olympic Games

The earliest connection between China and the Olympic Games was made at the time of the first Olympic Games. Pierre de Coubertin, founder of the modern Olympic movement and the first secretary-general of the International Olympic Committee at the time, wrote a letter to the government of the Qing Dynasty in 1894, inviting China to participate in the first modern Olympic Games held in Athens, Greece, in 1896. If this is the case, it can be said that Emperor Guangxu was the first Chinese individual to receive an Olympic invitation.

China missed the first Olympic Games because of domestic troubles and foreign invasion, but the Chinese sports lovers at home and abroad never gave up their pursuit of sports and the Olympic Games. Their interest in the Olympic Games began from the time of the Third Olympic Games held in St. Louis, the United States in 1904. Many Chinese newspapers and magazines carried reports on the Third Games, but it did not arouse any response for political, economic, cultural and educational factors. In October 1907, China's physical educationist Zhang Bailing suggested in his address at the fifth school games of the Young Men's Christian Association in Tianjin that China should also make preparations in the near future to participate in the Olympic Games. He stressed that many European countries sent their athletes to the Olympic Games although they had few chances of winning medals. In an article entitled "Competitive Sports" published in 1908, the journal *Tianjin Youth* put forward the suggestion that the Olympic Games could be hosted in China. This perhaps was the first time that any Chinese expressed the idea of hosting the Olympic Games in China. After 1910, China's first national games were held in Nanjing under the slogans of "Strive to participate in the Olympic Games in the near future" and "Strive to host the Olympic Games in China in the near future". This was the first fruit borne of the persistent pursuit of the Olympic Games by the Chinese people, but it was only a beginning.

In 1913, China participated in the Far East Games (also called as the Far East Olympic Games) as one of its initiators. The Games received recognition from the International Olympic Committee in 1915. As China actively organized and participated in the Far East Games, it had more contacts with the IOC. After recognizing the Far East Games, the IOC invited China to participate in the Sixth Olympic Games to be held in Berlin, Germany in 1916, but the Olympic dream did not come true for the Chinese people because of World War I. After Wang Zhengting, an official of the Northern Government, became a member of the IOC, China began its direct contact with the IOC. The National Sports Association was established in 1924, and China was also admitted into several international sports federations, including the athletic, swimming and gymnastics federations, as well as five other international sports federations. The IOC formally recognized the Chinese National Sports Federation as a member association in 1931. From then on, China had closer relations with the IOC, and participated in the major competitions organized by the IOC.

Wang Zhengting played a major role during these years. Born in Fenghua, Zhejiang Province, in 1882, he was a council member of the All-China Sports Promotion Association, and held important positions in the national sports organizations and in organizing important domestic and international competitions. He was also an initiator of the Far East Sports Association and one of the sponsors of the Far East Games. He was the president of the second, fifth and eighth Far East Games. In 1922, he was elected a member of the IOC, thus becoming China's first IOC member. As head of the Chinese delegation, he took part in the 11th Olympic Games in Berlin, Germany, in 1936 and the 14th Olympic Games in London, Britain, in 1948.

■The Chinese and the Olympic Games in the early 20th century

The first Chinese athlete to appear at the Olympic Games was Liu Changchun. Born in Dalian, Liaoning, in 1909, he was good at sprints with big and fast strides. He broke three national records in the 100m, 200m and 400m races at the 14th North China Games held in Shenyang from May 31st through June 2, 1929 by clocking 10.8 seconds, 22.4

seconds and 52.4 seconds respectively. His records were very encouraging. The 100m Olympic gold medal time at the 1928 Olympic Games held in Amsterdam was also 10.8 seconds. So far as his strength was concerned, he was already a world-class athlete.

The Chinese government made hasty entries at the 10th Olympic Games in 1932, and Liu Changchun was the athlete representing China. At the opening ceremony, Liu was the flag bearer at the head of the Chinese delegation, which included Shen Ciliang, secretary-general of the All-China Sports Association, coach Song Junfu, and some Chinese from Los Angeles, as well as a clerk from the YMCA.

As he had spent 25 days on a ship on the Pacific Ocean, Liu Changchun was very fatigued by the long journey. He failed to achieve good results on the track. Liu Changchun should have had the strength to be among the finalists in the 100m and 200m races, but he was eliminated in the heats for his fifth and sixth places. He was entered in the 400m race, but was too fatigued to appear in it. After the races, Liu Changchun found himself in an awkward situation as he had no money for the fare to travel back home. Later he managed to get home only because of the money donated by local Chinese.

Although Liu did not win a medal at the Olympics, nor did he even compete in the semi-finals, his presence represented the Chinese debut at the Olympics, and his appearance was of epoch-making significance in Chinese Olympic history. By his presence, he

Liu Changchùn failed to qualify for the semi-finals in the 1932 Olympic sprints

announced the existence of the Olympic Movement in China to the world.

Soon after Liu Changchun became the first Chinese athlete to appear in the competition arena of the Olympic Games, the Kuomintang government began to make preparations for participation in the 11th Olympic Games, issuing an order to the All-China Sports Association to select and train athletes.

In 1936, China sent an extraordinarily large sports delegation of several hundred people, including 63 athletes, along with coaches and staff members to the Olympic Games in Berlin, Germany. Chinese athletes competed in basketball, track and field, football, swimming, weightlifting, boxing and cycling, and demonstrated the Chinese martial arts. They arrived in Europe in the company of a 34-member sports study group. However, except for a pole vaulter who qualified for the semi-finals, all the athletes were eliminated in the preliminaries and heats. It is especially worthy of mention that a Chinese football team appeared for the first time in history at the Olympics. According to the draw, China played against Britain in the first round. The British team was a strong one in the world at that time and its players had outstanding skills and physique. The Chinese players knew that they had little chance of winning the match, but they played stubbornly with a 0:0 tie in the first half. Although the Chinese team lost the match 0:2 after 90 minutes of play, the players received favorable comments from the local press indicating that they demonstrated good personal skills and good teamwork. They lost mostly because they lacked good stamina and speed.

While the Chinese athletes were in an awkward and helpless position, the Chinese traditional martial artists captured particular attention within the world sports circles. This was a sign of their recognition of and respect for Chinese traditional sports and a comfort to Chinese sports lovers.

Before the Chinese football team had time to breathe and China had an opportunity to popularize its traditional martial arts to the world, World War II broke out, thus halting the organization of the 12th and 13th Olympic Games. After these two Olympiads, the 14th Olympic Games were held in London, Britain, in 1948. The All-China Sports Association sent 33 athletes to compete in basketball, football, track and field events, swimming and cycling. Only one athlete each was entered in swimming and cycling. At their own expense, Wu Chuanyu, a Chinese athlete living overseas in Indonesia competed in swimming, and He Haohua, a Chinese resident living in the Netherlands, competed in cycling. The Chinese delegation was so short of funds that they could not even cover their airline tickets for all participants. Both the basketball team and the football team played exhibition matches in Southeast Asian countries to earn money for their traveling costs. While all athletes from other countries lived in the Olympic Village, the financially strapped Chinese delegation was accommodated in the humble premises of a local primary school. He Haohua led the pack all the way in the road cycling race and was about to finish in the first place, but was knocked down by an overtaking cyclist and ended up with a serious bone fracture.

China had participated in the Olympic Games several times before the founding of the People's Republic of China in 1949, but had finished with undesirable results. This was a reflection of the underdeveloped politics, economy, culture and education in the country. The development of the modern economy is the social foundation for the modern Olympic movement in China, and this is an objective fact. If not for the dramatic change in the underdeveloped political and economic situation, it would have been very difficult for the Olympic movement in China to develop so quickly.

■New China's Journey to the Olympics

From the time that New China was founded to its capture of the first Olympic gold medal, namely during the period from 1949 to 1984, nine Olympic summer games and nine Olympic winter games were held, but China participated in only two summer Olympics and two winter Olympics. During this period, the Chinese Olympic Committee was forced to suspend its ties with the International Olympic Committee. Nevertheless, the Chinese athletes never gave up the goals and spirit of the Olympic movement, but contributed their positive efforts to the development of the Olympic movement within the scope of their own capabilities.

■The 15th Summer Olympics in 1952

The 15th Summer Olympics were held in Helsinki, Finland, in 1952. The Chinese delegation received an invitation cable from the Organizing Committee of the 15th Olympic Games only one day before the opening ceremony.

China quickly formed a 40-member delegation in the subsequent three or four days. The delegation included a 15-member men's football team, a 10-member men's basketball team, male swimmer Wu Chuanyu, interpreters, doctors and journalists. It was already noon on July 29 when the first Olympic delegation from New China arrived at the Olympic Village, and the Games were already starting to close down.

New China's national flag was raised for the first time at the Olympic Games in Helsinki.

Soon after the Chinese delegation arrived at the Olympic Village on the outskirts of Helsinki, it attended the flag-raising ceremony without first stopping to eat or rest. This was the first time that the five-starred red flag fluttered at the Olympic Games. Hundreds of athletes and journalists from other countries joined the Chinese delegation in a very friendly and amiable atmosphere. Rong Gaotang, chef de mission of the Chinese delegation, gave an enthusiastic address: "Although we are late, we are here after all. We have brought with us our desire for peace and friendship. We will meet athletes of all countries. We believe deeply that such meetings will enhance the mutual understanding and friendship between the athletes of China and the athletes from all other countries."

This was the first time the People's Republic of China made its voice heard at a global sports festival. It was also the first time that the national flag of New China was raised in the Olympic competition venue. The raising of the flag was also a way of proclaiming to the world: China has come to the Olympics.

China participated in the Helsinki Olympic Games, but most of the events had ended by the time the Chinese athletes arrived at the competition venues. Only Wu Chuanyu competed in the men's 100m backstroke heats on July 30. Affected by fatigue from a long flight and the time difference, he finished in 1 minute 12.3 seconds and was thus disqualified from the finals. This was the first record chalked up by a swimmer of China at the Olympics. With the extinction of the Olympic flame on August 3, China ended its first Olympic appearance in this way.

■Regaining the legitimate seat of the Chinese Olympic Committee in the IOC

In order to safeguard the reunification and integrity of Chinese territory, the Chinese Olympic Committee announced the severance of its ties with the IOC on August 19, 1958, and withdrew from 15 international sports federations between June and August of the same year. Dong Shouyi, then a Chinese member of the IOC, resigned from the

IOC. China was thus absent from many international sports competitions in the subsequent 22 years.

In 1972, China's legitimate seat in the United Nations was restored. In 1979, the Chinese Olympic Committee formally put forward its proposal to settle the question of China's legitimate seat to the International Olympic Committee. The proposal was accepted by most of the IOC members including Lord Killanin, the IOC President. In November the same year, the IOC made an arrangement for its members to vote by means of correspondence on a resolution to restore the legitimate seat of the People's Republic of China in the International Olympic Committee which had been made by the IOC Executive Board in Nagoya, Japan, on October 25, 1979. As a result, the resolution was adopted with 62 members for, 17 against, and two abstentions. The Nagoya resolution states that the Chinese Olympic Committee will use the national flag and national anthem of the People's Republic of China when it participates in the Olympic Games whereas Taiwan will be permitted to have seats in the international sports organizations as China's local organization and appear in the name of the Chinese Taipei Olympic Committee. The IOC's decision finally cleared the remaining obstacle preventing China's return to the Olympic family. Since then, the Chinese Olympic Committee and the International Olympic Committee have formed a good and close mutually cooperative relationship.

Between 1956 and 1979, the Chinese Olympic Committee did not send any representatives to the Olympic Games. However, Yang Chuan-kuang of Chinese Taipei won a silver medal in the decathlon at the 1960 Olympic Games in Rome, Italy. He became the first Chinese athlete to take an Olympic medal. Then at the 1968 Olympic Games held in Mexico City, Chi Cheng of Chinese Taipei won a bronze medal in the women's 80m hurdle, and was the first female Chinese athlete to win an Olympic medal.

■ The 13th Olympic Winter Games in Lake Placid, 1980

After having its seat restored on the International Olympic Committee, a sports delegation from the People's Republic of China made its first Olympic appearance by participating in the 13th Olympic Winter Games in Lake Placid, the United States, in February 1980. It had 28 athletes in 18 events in skating, skiing and biathlon. Wang Guizhen's 18th place in the women's slalom in the alpine skiing event was the best result a Chinese athlete had ever attained at that time. It was also a debut for the Chinese athletes at the Olympic Winter Games.

An end to zero
— China's first Olympic gold medal

Xu Haifeng, winner of China's first Olympic gold medal, likes to take photos in his free time.

In 1984, the Chinese Olympic delegation left Beijing by air in two groups on the 14th and 19th to participate in the 23rd Olympic Summer Games in Los Angeles. The delegation consisted of 225 athletes and 50 coaches and competed in 16 sports apart from football, hockey, boxing, equestrians, and modern pentathlon. Additionally, China also sent a group of retired sports officials and celebrities known within the sports circles, a group of journalists and a troupe of performing artists.

The Olympic Committee in Taipei signed an agreement with the International Olympic Committee in 1981, agreeing to participate in the Los Angeles Olympic Games under the name of "Chinese Taipei", and it sent 67 athletes to compete in track and field, swimming and weightlifting events. The Chinese athletes from the two sides of the Taiwan Strait met for the first time at the Olympic Games.

On July 29, the day after the opening ceremony, the first Olympic gold medal of the 23rd Olympic Games was won in the shooting events, and Chinese athletes Xu Haifeng and Wang Yifu participated in these events. However, no one had expected that this gold medal would become a medal of great historical significance — that it would be the first gold medal in Chinese Olympic history.

Xu Haifeng was the lucky person to bear this honor. He scored 566 points in the men's free pistol slow-fire to win the first gold medal for China in its history with Olympics, thus breaking China's record of having no gold medals.

■History of China's first Olympic gold medal

On July 29, 1984, the free pistol slow-fire event took place at the Olympic shooting range. The competitors were required to fire 60 shots in two and a half hours. The sharpshooters from different parts of the world stood at 80 shooting stations. At first, all the journalists and other people concentrated their attention on Ragnar Skanaker of Sweden, winner of the free pistol slow-fire gold medal at the 20th Olympic Games, and stood behind his station. After the referee gave the starting signal, when other shooters had already fired four or five shots, Xu Haifeng was not at all anxious, and was still repeating the movements of picking up his pistol and putting it down again. His first shot was fired five minutes after the starting signal. This abnormality caught the attention of the journalists and spectators behind him, and also aroused curiosity among the crowds. The Chinese athlete in a red T-shirt at the No. 40 station began to attract attention.

Xu was in good form after firing his 28th shot. He should have continued his shooting streak, but instead, he went to sit down for a rest.

One and a half hours passed. The Chinese journalists covering the event were all anxious, but they did not dare to disturb him. The crowds and journalists behind his station sighed.

In the last stage of the competition, Xu still had the last set of 10 shots to fire. When he scored two 10s and two 9s in the first four shots, he became a bit nervous, but he quickly recovered. The lapse again evoked sighs from the Chinese journalists and the crowds.

Xu sat in repose with his eyes closed to regain his composure. He then fired all the remaining shots except for one.

Xu and Skanaker were tied before the last shot was fired. The air around seemed to stagnate, and the people were awaiting the final results. Xu raised his pistol slowly, then put it down again. He raised it and put it down again. He repeated these movements four times. He knew very well what his last shot would mean. He finally fired his last shot, and scored a perfect 10, defeating the Swedish shooter by one point, and thus winning the gold medal.

Before Xu even had time to put down his firearm, the leader of the Chinese sports delegation rushed forward to hug him.

■The Chinese national anthem was played for the first time at the Olympics

After the end of the competition, all the people in the shooting range waited for the playing of the national anthem of the People's Republic of China for the first time in Olympic history as the national flag of China was hoisted. However, the medal awards ceremony had to be delayed.

It turned out that the officials of the shooting competition had expected that the Chinese shooters would produce good results, but they had never thought that they would win the gold medal, so they had only one Chinese national flag on hand. However, in the very first shooting event, there were two Chinese athletes among the top three, with Wang Yifu winning the bronze medal. According to Olympic rules, the first three finalists should all have their national flags hoisted, so another Chinese national flag was needed. The organizers had to send for another flag. Finally they found one where the national flags of competitors were stored. The medal awarding ceremony was thus delayed for an hour.

IOC President Juan Antonio Samaranch had said that he would personally award the first gold medal won by China. The results were not what he had anticipated. Therefore, he was not at the venue. He went to the shooting range immediately after hearing the news, and personally awarded the gold medal to Xu. He solemnly announced: "A Chinese athlete has won the first gold medal of the Olympic Games. This is the greatest day in Chinese sports history. I am honored to be able to personally award this gold medal to the Chinese shooter."

The winning of the first gold medal by Xu Haifeng was not a simple matter. The

The wax statue in the Chinese Waxworks Museum of Xu Haifeng shooting
for the first Olympic gold medal at the Los Angeles Olympic Games

first flag of the victor at the 23rd Olympic Games was the five-starred red flag of the People's Republic of China. This was also the first time that the Chinese national flag was
hoisted at the Olympics. The national anthem of the victor played was also the national
anthem of the People's Republic of China. It was also the first time that the national
anthem of the People's Republic of China had ever been heard at the Olympics. The
other first was even more significant. It had been the dream of Chinese people all over
the world for more than a half a century to break their "zero" gold medal record at the
Olympic Games. Their dream came true on July 29, 1984. This would become a date in
which the Chinese people would always take pride.

China's place in the medal tally and the world records it set at the Olympics |

Chinese athletes have participated in ten Olympic Summer Games (three before and seven after the founding of the People's Republic of China in 1949) and eight Olympic Winter Games between the time that China made its first appearance at the 10th Olympic Games in Los Angeles in 1932 and the 20th Olympic Winter Games held in Turin, Italy, in 2006. Beginning in 1984 when the Chinese Olympic athletes competed in the Los Angeles, the Chinese athletes have stirred up a "Chinese whirlwind" throughout the world. The following are tables of the medals that Chinese athletes have won and the world records they have set at the summer and winter Olympics.

Chinese athletes marching in at the opening ceremony of the 2004 Olympic Games in Athens, with Yao Ming as the bearer of the Chinese national flag

I. Summer Olympic Games

The medal count of the 23rd Olympic Games (1984, Los Angeles, USA)

Rank	Nation	Gold	Silver	Bronze	Total
1	United States	83	61	30	174
2	Romania	20	16	17	53
3	Federal Germany	17	19	23	59
4	China	15	8	9	32

Chen Zhong took the gold medal in the women's over 67kg weight category in tae kwon do at the 2004 Olympic Games in Athens.

The medal count of the 24th Olympic Games (1988, Seoul, Republic of Korea)

Rank	Nation	Gold	Silver	Bronze	Total
1	Soviet Union	55	31	46	132
2	Dem. Germany	37	35	30	102
3	United States	36	31	27	94
4	Republic of Korea	12	10	11	33
5	Federal Germany	11	14	15	40
6	Hungary	11	6	6	23
7	Bulgaria	10	12	13	35
8	Romania	7	11	6	24
9	France	6	4	6	16
10	Italy	6	4	4	14
11	China	5	11	12	28

The medal count of the 25th Olympic Games (1992, Barcelona, Spain)

Rank	Nation	Gold	Silver	Bronze	Total
1	Unified Team (ex-USSR)	45	38	29	112
2	United States	37	34	37	108
3	Germany	33	21	28	82
4	China	16	22	16	54

The medal count of the 26th Olympic Games (1996, Atlanta, USA)

Rank	Nation	Gold	Silver	Bronze	Total
1	United States	44	32	25	101
2	Russia	26	21	16	63
3	Germany	20	18	27	65
4	China	16	22	12	50

The world records broken by Chinese athletes at the 26th Olympic Games

Men's two-lift total in the 59kg category	307.5 kg	Tang Lingsheng
Men's snatch in the 70kg category	162.5 kg	Zhan Xugang
Men's jerk in the 70kg category	195 kg	Zhan Xugang
Men's two-lift total in the 70kg category	357.5 kg	Zhan Xugang
Women's individual archery elimination rounds overall score	330 points	Wang Xiaozhu
Women's team archery elimination rounds overall score	887 points	Wang Xiaozhu, He Ying & Yang Jianping

The medal count of the 27th Olympic Games (2000, Sydney, Australia)

Rank	Nation	Gold	Silver	Bronze	Total
1	United States	40	24	33	97
2	Russia	32	28	28	88
3	China	28	16	15	59

The world records broken by Chinese athletes at the 27th Olympic Games

Women's snatch in the 53kg category	110 kg	Yang Xia
Women's jerk in the 53kg category	122.5 kg	Yang Xia
Women's jerk in the 53kg category	125 kg	Yang Xia
Women's two-lift total in the 53kg category	222.5 kg	Yang Xia
Women's two-lift total in the 53kg category	225 kg	Yang Xia
Women's snatch in the 63kg category	112.5 kg	Chen Xiaomin
Women's two-lift total in the 63kg category	242.5 kg	Chen Xiaomin
Women's snatch in the over 75kg category	135 kg	Ding Meiyuan
Women's jerk in the over 75kg category	165 kg	Ding Meiyuan
Women's two-lift total in the over 75kg category	292.5 kg	Ding Meiyuan
Women's two-lift total in the over 75kg category	297.5 kg	Ding Meiyuan
Women's two-lift total in the over 75kg category	300 kg	Ding Meiyuan

The medal count of the 28th Olympic Games (2004, Athens, Greece)

Rank	Nation	Gold	Silver	Bronze	Total
1	United States	35	39	29	103
2	China	32	17	14	63
3	Russia	27	27	38	92

The world records broken by Chinese athletes at the 28th Olympic Games

Men's air rifle shooting (10m)	702.7 points	Zhu Qinan
Women's snatch in the 69kg category	122.5 kg	Liu Chunhong
Women's jerk in the 69kg category	152.5 kg	Liu Chunhong
Women's two-lift total in the 69kg category	275 kg	Liu Chunhong
Women's jerk in the +75kg category	182.5kg	Tang Gonghong
Women's two-lift total in the +75kg category	305 kg	Tang Gonghong

above: Du Li, a female Olympic champion in the air rifle event

right: Li Ting and Sun Tiantian, women's tennis doubles champion at the 2004 Olympic Games in Athens,Greece

■ II. Olympic Winter Games

The medal count of the 15th Olympic Winter Games
(1988, Calgary, Canada)

The Chinese delegation took two gold medals and one bronze medal in the women's short track demonstration events at the 1988 Olympic Winter Games in Calgary.

The world records set by Chinese athlete at the 15th Olympic Winter Games in Calgary

Women's 1500m short track	2 min 34.85 sec	Li Yan
Women's 1000m short track	1 min 39 sec	Li Yan

The medal count of the 16th Olympic Winter Games
(1992, Albertville, France)

Rank	Nation	Gold	Silver	Bronze	Total
1	Germany	10	10	6	26
2	Unified Team	9	6	8	23
3	Norway	9	6	5	20
15	China	0	3	0	3

The medal count of the 17th Olympic Winter Games
(1994, Lillehammer, Norway)

Rank	Nation	Gold	Silver	Bronze	Total
1	Russia	11	8	4	23
2	Norway	10	11	5	26
3	Germany	9	7	8	24
19	China	0	1	2	3

The medal count of the 18th Olympic Winter Games (1998, Nagano, Japan)

Rank	Nation	Gold	Silver	Bronze	Total
1	Germany	12	9	8	29
2	Norway	10	10	5	25
3	Russia	9	6	3	18
16	China	0	6	2	8

The world record set by Chinese athlete at the 18th Olympic Winter Games

Women's 1000m short track	1 min 31.991 sec	Yang Yang

The medal count of the 19th Olympic Winter Games
(2002, Salt Lake City, USA)

Rank	Nation	Gold	Silver	Bronze	Total
1	Norway	13	5	7	25
2	Germany	12	16	8	36
3	United States	10	13	11	34
13	China	2	2	4	8

The medal count of the 20th Olympic Winter Games (2006, Turin, Italy)

Rank	Nation	Gold	Silver	Bronze	Total
1	Germany	11	12	6	29
2	United States	9	9	7	25
3	Austria	9	7	7	23
14	China	2	4	5	11

Shen Xue and Zhao Hongbo in the
pairs figure skating competition

China's strong Olympic sports |

Among the 28 sports at the Olympic Summer Games, China is traditionally strong in table tennis, diving, gymnastics, shooting, weightlifting and badminton.

■Table Tennis

Table tennis is known as China's "national ball game." This title was not self-designated, but was earned after years of hard work by the Chinese table tennis players. Since 1988 when table tennis was first admitted as an Olympic sport up until 2004, the Olympic Games produced 20 gold medals. China took 16 of them, leaving only four to players of other countries (3 to Korea and 1 to the "evergreen tree" Jan-Ove Waldner of Sweden at the 1992 Barcelona Olympic Games). The Chinese team made a clean sweep of the gold medals both at the Atlanta and Sydney games, and was worthy of the name of "dream team." In order to break the Chinese domination in the world, the International Olympic Committee has taken many measures, first to change the small ball to a bigger ball, and then to change the 21-point system to an 11-point system, and it has also introduced overt service in place of covert service. All these measures were intended to restrict the Chinese monopoly over the sport.

The long-standing domination of Chinese players in this world sport is due to the fact that the Chinese table tennis players have undergone arduous training, have been making persistent efforts to make improvements, and have been united as one person. From Rong Guotuan who won the first men's singles title for China in 1959 to Deng Yaping who dominated the women's sport for many years, and from Zhuang Zedong with the nickname of "young tiger" to Wang Nan popularly known as a "fake boy," the Chinese table tennis players have won many honors for their country. So far as a single sport is concerned, the popularity of table tennis in China is unmatched by other sports. It even holds a special place in Chinese political life and the national spirit.

In October 1952, the All-China Sports Federation organized a national table tennis championships in Beijing. Nineteen players were selected from among the participants and began their intensive training in Beijing in preparation for the Asian Championships in Singapore and the 20th World Championships in Romania. This marked the beginning of the Chinese table tennis teams' expeditions to the sports arenas of the world. The players, who had fewer than six months of training, participated in the world championships and made their first appearance on the world table tennis stage in Romania.

The 23rd World Championships were opened in Tokyo, Japan, April 1956. China's leading player was Jiang Yongning, who defeated Johnny Leach, twice world champion, when China met England in a team match. He was the first Chinese athlete to beat a world champion in the world championships. Rong Guotuan snatched the first world championship title for China in the World Championships in Germany in 1959, bringing home the St. Bride Trophy. It was an unprecedented honor in the sports history of China. From this time on, Chinese table tennis began to capture national attention and to gain in national popularity.

The 26th World Table Tennis Championships took place in Beijing in 1961. This was the most significant international sports competition ever hosted by China. China took three of the seven world titles: the men' team, men's singles and women's singles, thus laying the foundation for China's supremacy in world table tennis.

The 1960s marked the first peak period for Chinese table tennis. At the 27th World Championships held two years later, the Chinese players captured the men's team title, sweeping the first four places in the men's singles and the first three places in

Wang Liqin, China's famous table tennis player

the men's doubles. At the 28th World Championships in 1965, China took five gold medals. This was the best performance ever achieved by the Chinese table tennis team since it first began to participate in the world championships. China, however, was absent from the 29th and 30th World Table Tennis Championships.

The 31st World Table Tennis Championships were held in Nagoya, Japan, March 1971. After a six-year absence, the Chinese table tennis team reappeared at the Championships. It took the women's singles, women's doubles and the mixed doubles titles, and started China's "ping pong diplomacy."

Zhuang Zedong, five-time Chinese winner of the St. Bride Trophy, joined Boggan, a player on the U.S. team who visited China in 1971, at a party celebrating the 35th anniversary of the "Ping Pong Diplomacy" between China and the United States.

On April 6, 1971, the Chinese table tennis team, which was participating in the World Championships, sent an invitation to the U.S. table tennis team to visit China. On April 10, 1971, the U.S. team and a small group of U.S. journalists became the first Americans to be permitted to enter China since the People's Republic of China was founded in 1949. On April 10, Zhou Enlai, then premier of China, received the members of the U.S. team and told them: "You have started a new chapter in the relations between the Chinese people and the people of the United States. I believe that the beginning of our friendship will surely be supported by the majority of the peoples of our two countries."

Hours after Zhou Enlai's statement, President Nixon of the United States announced a number of measures to lift the ban on China. In return, the U.S. table tennis team invited the Chinese team to visit the United States, and the invitation was accepted immediately. On April 11, 1972, the Chinese table tennis team visited the United States, stopping first in Detroit. The mutual visits of the Chinese and U.S. table tennis teams created a sensation in the world press, and became a major event capturing the attention of the world. The "ping pong diplomacy" put an end to the 22-year suspension of exchanges of people between the two countries, thus marking a historical step toward the easing of tensions in the relations between China and the United States. This also brought about a huge change on the international scene. Table tennis thus earned the reputation of "using a small ball to move the earth."

At the writing of this book, the Chinese table tennis team had brought home altogether more than 100 world champion titles, making clean sweeps at three World Championships and two clean sweeps at the Olympic Games. The Chinese table tennis team has become an undisputed leader in world sports. Even when there have been some upsets at this or that particular championship game, the Chinese table tennis team has been able to find the most effective way to cope with any obstacles in the shortest period of time. The team has provided many classical examples in respect to the myths of invincibility. The emergence of the star players in the sport has exerted a far-reaching influence in sports and even in other fields in China.

Zhang Yining of the Chinese Table Tennis Team

Ma Lin and Chen Qi took the men's doubles at the 2004 Olympic Games in Athens.

█Diving

China won six of the eight gold medals in diving at the 2004 Olympic Games in Athens, thus setting a new gold winning record in the Chinese diving sport at Olympics, and bringing China's diving gold total to 20 in its 20 years of Olympic competition. With its dazzling successes, the Chinese diving team has established a strong position in world sports.

China began to cut a striking figure in the diving world in the 1980s. After Zhou Jihong won China's first Olympic diving gold medal in the women's platform event in Los Angeles in 1984, Chinese diving stars began to emerge one after another. Xu Yanmei and Gao Ming took two gold medals at the 1988 Olympic Games in Seoul. Two new stars, Fu Mingxia and Sun Shuwei, captivated the crowds in Barcelona in 1992. At the Atlanta Olympics in 1996, Xiong Ni, who distinguished himself by astonishing the diving world at the age of 14, proved his worth by winning his first Olympic gold medal. In addition, Fu Mingxia took another two gold medals for China in Atlanta.

Chinese divers Guo Jingjing and Wu Mingxia won the 3m women's pairs springboard event at the 2004 Olympic Games in Athens.

With Xiong Ni and Fu Mingxia retiring after the Atlanta Games, the Chinese sport of diving declined to an all-time low with the new divers losing one gold after another at the Grand Prix, World Cup and World Championships to the quickly emerging diving stars from Russia. In view of the fact that the new divers were still unable to challenge the Russians, the team's managers had no choice but to decide to recall both Xiong Ni and Fu Mingxia to the team to resume their training and to give encouragement to the young divers. As a result, the Chinese team won five of the eight gold medals in Sydney in 2000 after four synchronized diving events were first added to the Olympic program. China's newcomer Tian Liang defeated Russia's Atlanta Olympic Champion Dmitry Sautin for the gold medal in the men's platform event. Both Xiong Ni and Fu Mingxia fulfilled the expectations of the Chinese people by each taking an Olympic gold medal, thus bringing their respective diving careers to a perfect end.

The Chinese diving team won six gold medals at the Athens Olympics in 2004, demonstrating to the world that it was still a strong team continuing to make history.

Two Chinese women divers in competition

■Gymnastics

Since retiring as a gymnast, Li Ning has served as a member of the jury for many international gymnastic competitions.

At the 1984 Olympic Games in Los Angeles, Chinese gymnast Li Ning alone won three gold medals, marking the beginning of the participation of Chinese gymnasts in the gymnastic world. Subsequently, Li Ning, Li Xiaoshuang and Li Xiaopeng also took gold medals at the Olympic Games. Hence, they came to be known by the popular designation of "fighters of Li's family."

China had a poor foundation and a low level of competition when it started to develop artistic gymnastics. After numerous twists and turns in the course of the development, the country began to reap the first fruits of its labor and joined the leading gymnastic nations in the 1980s. At the World Cup Gymnastic Tournament held in Toronto, Canada, 1980, Li Yuejiu won the men's parallel bars while Huang Yubin tied with the Soviet gymnast Makuts for the gold medal in the rings. Zhu Zheng placed third in the women's uneven bars.

At the 21st World Championships held in Moscow in November 1981, the Chinese women's team placed second while the men's team placed third in the team events. Li Yuejiu and Koroliev of the Soviet Union tied for the first place in the men's floor exercises while Li Xiaoping tied with M. Nicola of the German Democratic Republic for the men's pommel horse gold medal. At the 6th World Cup Gymnastics Competition in October 1982, Li Ning won the men's all-around title and five of the six apparatus events, and has been subsequently cited as the world's second best gymnast. At the 22nd World Championships in 1983, the Chinese men's team defeated the world strongest team — the Soviet team, to take the team title and capture gold medals in the men's floor exercises and parallel bars, and thereby shocking the gymnastic world.

At the 23rd Olympic Games in Los Angeles in 1984, China won the silver medal in the men's team event and the bronze medal in the women's team event, with Li Ning capturing three gold medals in the floor exercises, pommel horse and rings, Lou Yun taking the gold medal in the men's vaulting horse event and Ma Yanhong winning in the women's uneven bars. In November of the same year, for the first time, the International Gymnastic Federation announced four original movements named after Chinese gymnasts: the Li Yuejiu somersault in floor exercise (1½ side flip and ¼ turn with a forward roll), the Tong Fei travel

The graceful posture of a Chinese woman gymnast

in pommel horse (circle with turn layout from end to end), the Li Ning handstand on parallel bars (giant circle with ½ turn to handstand), and the Li Ning mount in rings (back hang with arms extended and swing forward to L support, half level). Before the 23rd Olympic Games, the FIG held its 62nd congress and elected its new leading body. Because of the rapid improvement in Chinese gymnastics and China's rising international reputation, Zhang Quande was elected a FIG vice president, and Feng Jibai was elected vice chairman of the men's technical commission.

In recent years, the Chinese gymnastics have not been as good as they were in the 1980s, but still one of the world's strong gymnastic powers, China has continued to show its strength. It took one gold medal in 1996, two in 2000, and one gold medal at the 2004 Olympic Games.

Nineteen-year-old Teng Hai-bin won the men's pommel horse gold for China at the Athens Olympic Games in 2004.

▉Shooting

Shooting in China has been a popular sport and also one of China's strongest Olympic sports.

Chinese shooters Xu Haifeng, Li Yuwei and Wu Xiaoxuan captured three gold medals in the men's 50m slow-fire pistol, men's 50m standard-fire running target and women's 50m, 3×20 standard rifle at the 23rd Olympic Games in Los Angeles in 1984 with 566 points, 587 points and 581 points respectively.

At the Athens Games in 2004, the Chinese shooting team took 4 gold medals, 2 silver and 3 bronze medals, its best Olympic showing since 1984.

The graceful posture of a Chinese female shooter

China's shooting strength is roughly divided into three categories. In the first category are the strongest events in which Chinese shooters have absolute strength and have exhibited excellent performances in recent years, such as the women's 10m air pistol event, the women's 10m air rifle competition and the women's 25m sport pistol team event. The Chinese shooters are very confident about winning gold medals in these events at major international competitions. In the second category are the events in which Chinese shooters have no absolute strength but have shown steady improvement in recent years, such as the men's 10m air rifle event. In the third category are the events in which Chinese shooters had better strength in the past but have had no outstanding performances in recent years. However, as China was once superior and achieved brilliant results in these events, it has considerable experience and its coaches and athletes have ready training methods. These events include the women's double trap and the women's 3×20 small-bore rifle. Apart from these events, China has showed considerable strength in the men's running target event.

Wang Yifu, a veteran Olympic shooter

■ Weightlifting

China holds 18 of the 21 world records in the women's weightlifting divisions. Since the Los Angeles Olympics, Chinese weightlifters have brought home 18 Olympic gold medals at four out of five Olympic Games, with the exception being Barcelona where Chinese weightlifters took no gold medals. In the men's lighter weight category, Chinese weightlifters have for a long time stood among the front-runners in the world,

having set many world records in the 56kg to 77kg categories, and one after the other have become world or Olympic champions. Chinese weightlifters took all the gold medals in the four lighter weight divisions at the 1984 Olympic Games, and at the subsequent Olympics five gold medals were awarded to Chinese male weightlifters, all in the lighter and middle

In the training hall of the Chinese weightlifting team

weight divisions. Zhan Xugang captured the gold medals in the 77kg division at both the Atlanta and Sydney Olympics in 1996 and 2000. He was the first Chinese athlete to become a defending champion in weightlifting at the Olympics.

In Athens, 2004, five Chinese athletes — Chen Yanqing, Liu Chunhong, Tang Gonghong, Shi Zhiyong and Zhang Guozheng — won gold medals in weightlifting. The emergence of the upcoming young weightlifters has provided an adequate supply of promising champions for the Chinese weightlifting team. In particular, there are a good number of talented weightlifters in the men's 56kg division, including world record-setters in the snatch and jerk events. In the men's 77kg division, China also has weightlifters with strength matching the world's best weightlifters. Moreover, the men's 62kg division boasts a number of young weightlifters represented by Qiu Le. In the women's 48kg division, Wang Mingjuan and Yang Lian are both world record-setters. In the women's 53kg division in which China once lost a gold medal, Li Ping is now a new world record holder.

Chinese lifter Shi Zhiyong won a gold medal in the men's 62kg division at the Athens Olympic Games in 2004

■Badminton

Of the 19 Olympic badminton gold medals won so far, China took eight, ranking first in the Olympic gold medal tally in the sport, followed by Indonesia and the Republic of Korea with five gold medals each, and Denmark, third, with one.

Badminton became an official Olympic sport at the Barcelona Games in 1992. In Barcelona, there were only four events for badminton, the men's and women's singles and the men's and women's doubles, similar to other racket games. In the end, Indonesia took both the men's and women's singles gold medals while South Korea captured the gold medals in the men's and women's doubles.

In 1996, Ge Fei and Gu Jun won an Olympic gold medal for the Chinese team in the women's doubles. This marked the beginning of Chinese supremacy in world badminton. In 2000, China swept all the four gold medals in Sydney. At the Olympic Games in Athens in 2004, Chinese players won three gold medals in the women's singles and doubles and the mixed doubles. Although there was one fewer gold medal in 2004, it was still more than enough to show China's leading position in the badminton world.

At present, China has a splendid collection of badminton stars. Lin Dan, Chen Hong, Bao Chunlai and Fu Haifeng are in the men's elite while Gong Ruina, Zhang Ning, Zhou Mi, Gao Ling, Huang Sui, Wei Yili and Zhao Tingting are among the women's best.

above: Bao Chunlai, a young and promising Chinese badminton player

below: Zhang Ning won the gold medal in the women's singles at the 2004 Olympic Games in Athens

Capturing gold medals at the Olympics |

■Li Ning — Gymnastic Giant

(Olympic Champion in the floor exercise, pommel horse and rings at the 23rd Olympic Games in Los Angeles)

The first Chinese athlete to win six gold medals at a major world gymnastics tournament was Li Ning, and the first Chinese athlete to win three gold medals at one Olympic Games was also Li Ning. Li is the Chinese athlete who has won the greatest number of gold medals in international gymnastics tournaments, bagging a total of 64 gold medals in 24 tournaments starting with the Sino-US contest in 1981 and ending with the American Cup in 1988.

Li seized six gold medals in the all-round, floor exercise, pommel horse, rings, vaulting horse and horizontal bar at the Sixth World Cup in 1982, adding a miraculous chapter to the Chinese history of gymnastics. It was also the first such feat recorded in the international history of gymnastics. At the 23rd Olympic Games in Los Angeles two years later, he again won three gold medals in the floor exercise, pommel and rings plus two silver medals and one bronze medal, contributing to one-fifth of the Olympic medals received by the Chinese Olympic Delegation. Li was the athlete winning the greatest number of Olympic medals from among all the Chinese athletes in Los Angeles. In the World Cup Competition in Beijing in 1986, he won three gold medals in the all-round, floor exercise and pommel.

However, Li's gymnastic career ended in 1988 when he was unsuccessful at the 24th Olympic Games in Seoul. When performing his routine at the rings, Li unexpectedly fell. He walked down from the podium with his usual smile, but when he returned to the Beijing International Airport, he walked alone through an unnoticed corridor, looking dejected because of missing the opportunity to win an Olympic gold medal. Not long after this happened, Li announced his retirement at the age of 26.

Li was born into a teacher's family in Liuzhou, Guangxi, southern China, in 1963. He started studying gymnastics at the age of seven, and became a member of the national team at 17. He collected a total of 106 gold medals at the major national and international tournaments during his 18 years of gymnastic life. Among them, he won 92 national championships and 14 world championships. The

Li Ning performing on the pommel horse in Los Angeles in 1984

International Gymnastics Federation named some of his original movements after him, such as the Li Ning Parallel Bar, the Li Ning Pommel Horse, Li Ning 1 and Li Ning 2. In 1999, he was named one the world's best athletes of the 20th century. His name is included among the 25 athletic giants of the century, together with heavyweight boxing champion Muhammad Ali of the United States, soccer star Pele of Brazil and cager Michael Jordan of the United States.

■Xiong Ni — an Eight-year Dream

(Men's 3m springboard champion in Atlanta, men's 3m springboard champion and men's 3m synchronized springboard champion in Sydney)

Everyone who is interested in the Olympic Games knows that Xiong Ni, a 14-year-old Chinese diver, lost to the defending champion Greg Louganis of the United States by a small fraction of a point only because of the latter's reputation with the jury at the 24th Olympic Games in Seoul in 1988.

Afterwards, the American diver announced his retirement, and the Chinese press proclaimed that "Xiong Ni's era is coming."

At the 1992 Olympic Games in Barcelona, it had been generally believed that Xiong Ni would win the springboard event, but again he lost because of an error in the last dive. But this time, he lost to younger teammate Sun Shuwei. He received only a bronze medal. The 18-year old diver was in his prime that year, and had captured gold medals in all the major international tournaments, but not the Olympic gold medal.

His two Olympic failures were a serious mental blow for Xiong Ni. He even entertained the idea of retirement. Under the influence of his coach, he came to appreciate the level of cruelty inherent in the competitive arena, and again braced himself to try for an Olympic gold medal for the third time.

Tan Liangde, a veteran diver, retired, and Xiong Ni accepted the new challenge. The manager of the diving team decided that he would receive training for both the springboard and platform events. From this moment on, he eagerly looked forward to the arrival of the Atlanta Games. He even dreamed of winning both the platform and the springboard events to become a double winner. However, fate was teasing the gold-thirsty young man. Just as Xiong was undergoing intensive training, he had a knee joint injury which confined him to bed for a long time. He was struck another blow. While preparing for the World Cham-

Xiong Ni and his teammate Xiao Hailiang won the synchronized springboard gold at the Sydney 2000.

pionships earlier, Xiong had already suffered a bone fracture after slipping while descending a slippery staircase. He had endured acute pain during the training period and had participated in the World Championships despite his injury. As a result, the bone fracture had not healed well and his back muscles were stiffened with a crack. Although Xiong eventually recovered from his injuries, he still had fears about participating in the platform event. He made it through the difficult period of the selective tests for the Atlanta Olympics. Considering his physical condition, the leaders of the diving team asked him to choose between the platform and the springboard. Xiong chose the springboard.

Xiong Ni in a torch relay for the 10th National Games

When he finally stood on the springboard to start his performance in the Atlanta diving pool, reminiscences of his old Olympic experiences were so clear to him that it was as if Seoul and Barcelona had just happened to him. This time in Atlanta, Xiong decided to take a low-profile stance as a newcomer. As expected, he was very relaxed in the finals, and performed according to form. At last, he managed to fulfill his dream of winning his first Olympic gold medal in the homeland of Greg Louganis, and put an end to the history of the Chinese male divers having never won an Olympic medal in the springboard event. It took eight years for Xiong to fulfill his dream for an Olympic gold medal.

Xiong appeared again at the Sydney Olympic Games in 2000, where he won the men's springboard gold medal and the men's synchronized springboard gold medal. He surpassed himself again and again in his 12-year diving career to truly become a person of great courage.

Born in Changsha, Hunan Province, January 1974, at the age of seven Xiong was enrolled in a sports school during his spare time. He started diving training under the tutelage of trainer Ma Yanping. In December 1984, he was selected to be a member of the Hunan provincial diving team. Xiong made rapid improvement thanks to his hard work and eagerness to learn. In April 1986, he made a clean sweep of the gold medals in the one-meter board, three-meter board, platform and three-event total to become the superstar in the Division B competition of the National Diving Championships in Nanjing. Beginning in 1988, Xiong became the only Chinese athlete to have participated in four Olympic Games and to have won medals. He is also an athlete of Hunan origin with the most world champion titles.

■Fu Mingxia — Diving Queen

(Platform champion at the 25th Olympic Games in Barcelona, double gold winner in the platform and springboard events at the 26th Olympic Games in Atlanta, and winner of the springboard gold at the 27th Olympic Games in Sydney)

Perfect and graceful was the dive performed by a small girl with a slim body from take-off, twist and turn, to entry with little splash in the women's springboard competition at the 25th Olympic Games in Barcelona. The girl was Fu Mingxia and only 14 years old when she won her first Olympic gold medal. Her dive produced a long, thunderous ovation from the stands and received a unanimous high score from all members of the jury. With her gold medal in hand as she had desired, she became the youngest champion in Olympic history.

As a matter of fact, Fu became the youngest world champion at the 6th World Swimming Championships the previous year when she won the gold medal in the women's platform event at the age of 13. This fact was recorded in the Guinness World Records. Fu not only won favor among the judges and crowds, but also received favorable comments from the inter-

The world famous diver Fu Mingxia

national press. The *Washington Post* wrote: "Dropping off the platform, she seemed to stop time…. It's as though she loves the air, and wants to stay in it." The front cover of the U.S. *Time* magazine was devoted to Fu's great dive after take-off above the skyline.

Fu achieved further successes when she won gold medals for both the platform and springboard events in Atlanta four years later to become the only double diving champion in recent Olympic history.

Fu retired after the 8th National Games in 1997, but she was recalled in 1999. In early March of the following year, she again became a member of the national team and resumed intensive training. At a selective contest in mid-April, Fu consolidated her position. She made her third appearance in the Sydney Games in September 2000, where she won the women's springboard gold medal and paired with Guo Jingjing to win the women's synchronized springboard gold medal.

Born in Wuhan, Hubei Province, 1978, she entered the gymnastics class of the Wuhan Municipal Sports School in 1985. She was later transferred to study diving, and became a member of the Hubei provincial diving team in 1987. When she was 12 years old and 1.37 meters tall in 1990, Fu won the platform gold medal in the Division B at the national junior championships. Soon afterwards, she was selected to be a member of the national diving team and undergo intensive training. This marked the beginning of her diving career. She finally retired after the Sydney Games and now resides in Hong Kong.

◾Liu Xiang — Asia's Flying Man

(Winner of the gold medal for the 110m hurdle at the 28th Olympic Games in Athens)

The Chinese Olympic expedition to Athens turned a 21-year-old big boy with a beaming face into a young man who rewrote the Chinese and even the world history of athletics.

Prior to the Olympic Games in Athens, no Chinese athlete had ever won a gold medal in the sprints at the Olympic Games. However, 21-year-old Liu Xiang, a big boy from Shanghai, changed history and wrote a brilliant chapter for China in the world history of track and field.

On August 27, 2004, Liu took his mark at the starting line of the home straight in the Olympic Stadium in Athens, and finished the men's hurdles race in 12.91 seconds to snatch the gold medal and match the previous world record held by Colin Jackson of the United States since 1993. He broke the Olympic record of 12.95 seconds set by Alan Johnson of the United States at the 1996 Olympic Games.

His best time prior to the Athens Olympics was 13.06 seconds. It was assumed that Liu would have no problem qualifying for the finals. He had even run the race within 13 seconds in one of his training tests. Despite this, his coach Sun Haiping had never

Liu Xiang in his training session at the Xinzhuang training site in Shanghai

relaxed his efforts to urge Liu to work still harder in preparing for the Games. Sun prepared a detailed training schedule suited to Liu's condition for the two months before leaving for the Greek capital city. In Liu's own words, "It was two unforgettable months." It was unforgettable because during those two months the amount of physical exertion was sometimes more or less beyond his endurance capacity. Usually, an athlete will vomit after intensive training. During those two months, Liu more than once very much wanted to vomit at the end of his training session. The reason why he could persevere in continuing to improve his performances was his conviction, a conviction to seize hold of the opportunity before him. The professional career of an athlete is limited, and it was the dream of this athlete to be able to reach his potential during his prime years. He knew well that the Olympic Games were held once every four years, and that he was still young, but changes could take place, and no one could predict what the future would bring. How many periods of four years could his athletic life span?

At 21:35 hours, Athens time on August 24, 2004, Liu placed first with a time of 13.27 seconds in heat. It could be clearly seen that when he was making his final spurt, Liu slowed down his pace a bit. He was apparently not at his best, because he wanted to retain his strength for the final race. In the next two rounds, he ran the races in 13.26 seconds and 13.18 seconds respectively.

At 21:30 hours on August 27, the Olympic stadium was filled with a capacity crowd waiting to see the 110m hurdle race.

Liu was ready for the final, standing at the starting line. The announcement was made that: "Liu Xiang, China, runs in the fourth lane." He looked very calm. As the starter fired the signal, the Brazilian hurdler in the 8th lane signaled to the starting judge, requesting a restart. Then, a U.S. hurdler made a false start. All the finalists were called back to the starting line.

After two false starts, the crowds became very excited, but Liu remained calm, without showing any sign of the pressure he must have been feeling.

When the starting pistol sounded for the third time, the eight finalists flew forward like arrows leaving strings of a bow. Liu ran very fast, leading. After jumping all the hurdles, he was the first to breast the finishing tape and win the gold medal. Liu Xiang won! Liu Xiang was the Olympic champion! Liu Xiang took the first place!

Tens of thousands of spectators in the stands at the stadium gave Liu a thunderous ovation. Liu ran a lap of honor, with the red five-starred national flag held high behind his back. The Chinese spectators in the stands were all jubilant and had tears in their

Liu Xiang won the 110m hurdle race with a new world record time of 12.88 seconds at the Super Track and Field Grand Prix in Lausanne, Switzerland, July 11, 2006.

eyes. They waved their national flags, shouting: "Liu Xiang, a good chap!"

His name was announced in the broadcast when the medal-awarding ceremony took place. Liu mounted the podium. He Zhenliang, a prestigious Chinese IOC member, presented the gold medal, and shed tears as he hung the gold medal around Liu's neck. At that moment, the whole stadium was cheering him on.

Born in Shanghai on July 13, 1983, Liu started to run the hurdle race in 1995. In the following year, he won the championship in the B Division at the Shanghai municipal junior track and field meet. Liu is 1.9 meters tall, and weighs 78 kilograms. He has a good build, a strong explosive force and an absolute speed. On August 28, 2001, he won his first world championship title — champion at the World University Students Games in Beijing. At the Grand Prix in Switzerland a year later, he began to display his talent when he broke the world youth record by clocking 13.12 seconds.

At the super track and field Grand Prix in Lausanne in Switzerland on July 11, 2006, Liu clocked 12.88 seconds to beat the 13-year-old world record holder in the 110m hurdle and win the gold medal. After the race, the excited Chinese athlete said: "I really can't believe it. This is a historical moment. I was the only Asian athlete who was able to defeat all my American and European counterparts at the Olympic Games."

Liu Xiang and the winners of the silver and bronze medals on the podium

Liu Xiang running a lap of honor with the five-starred red flag held behind his back after winning the race

■Wang Junxia — Miraculous Deer in the East

(Winner of the women's 5,000m race at the 26th Olympic Games in Atlanta)

Wang Junxia was born in the countryside in suburban Dalian City in Liaoning Province, Jaunary 9, 1973. Because of the difficult living conditions at home, since childhood she had acquired the fine qualities of enduring hardships and working hard. She was admitted to the Dalian Sports School in 1988 and starting her training in long-distance running. She became a member of the Liaoning provincial track and field team in 1991 and began to receive training under the well-known coach Ma Junren. After

intensive scientific and systematic training, Wang improved her physical qualities and running skills tremendously, and gradually acquired her own technical style of desired stride, quick stride frequency and powerful ability to make the final spurt. She won the 10,000m race at the Third World Youth Track and Field Championships by clocking 32 minutes 29.90 seconds in 1992, and won the silver medal in the juniors group at the 20th World Cross-country Championships in the same year.

Wang reached her climax in 1993 when she won the 10,000m race at the 4th World Track and Field Championships and the 5th World Cup Marathon Race. At the 7th National Games, she beat the 3,000m world record twice by clocking 8 minutes and 12.19 seconds and 8 minutes 6.11 seconds respectively, and smashed the women's 10,000m world record with a winning time of 29 minutes 31.78 seconds to become the first woman in the world to run 10,000m within 30 minutes. Wang thus became famed as the "miraculous deer in the east."

Wang Junxia running the 5,000m race in Atlanta in 1996 to take the gold medal

Her two world records have remained unbeaten up until today.

Wang made her Olympic debut
at the Atlanta Games in 1996. She
did not feel well before the race
began, but nevertheless the leaders
of the Chinese delegation hoped
that she would take one of the gold
medals in her races. Unexpectedly,
Wang appeared in the 5,000m race,
without the slightest sign of giving
up. She tried her best to run to the
finish. No one had expected that the
ill girl would win the gold medal in
the end. As no one had expected her
to be the first, there were no flowers

Olympic champion Wang Junxia becoming an image ambassador for the Olympic Fitness Road in Shenyang, Liaoning
Province

or national flags ready for her. She then took a national flag from a young man who was
waving it in the stands near the finish line, and excitedly began to run her lap of honor,
signaling to the world: A Chinese girl won the 5,000m Olympic gold medal! All the
Chinese spectators in the stands and those watching TV at home shared her honor at that
moment. On August 2, Wang again won a silver medal in the women's 10,000m race in
31 minutes 2.58 seconds.

In January 1997, the US magazine *Track and Field* picked her as one of the best
athletes in the world for 1996.

■The Chinese Women's Volleyball Team — Volleyball Elite

(Champion at the 23rd Olympic Games in Los Angeles and again the 28th
Olympic Games in Athens)

From the time of the Olympic Games in Los Angeles in 1984 to the Olympic Games
in Athens in 2000, the Chinese women's volleyball team won two gold medals, one silver medal, one bronze medal, came 5th place in one event and 7th place in another event.

Chinese women players hugging in excitement at winning the final match in Athens, 20 years after the Chinese team first winning the Olympic title

Prior to the Olympic Games in Los Angeles in 1984, the Chinese women's volleyball team had been the champions at the World Cup in Japan in 1981 and at the World Championship in Peru in 1982. This made the Chinese people place high hopes on their first Olympic appearance. The target of the players and their coach was to win their third world crown in succession.

Although the Soviet Union, Cuba and some East European countries did not participate in the Olympics, China, Peru, the United States and Japan, who took the first four places in the World Championships, were all present. The Chinese team beat both Brazil and Federal Germany 3:0 without any difficulty in the group, but lost to the host team, China's main rival, 1:3 as the players were too pressured and were overanxious to win. Because of their loss to the U.S. team, they had to meet Japan, a fairly strong team, in one of the semi-finals. Luckily, the Chinese girls were fully prepared and in high spirits, and beat the Japanese team easily 3:0 to meet the Americans again in the final. The Chinese-American encounter was most thrilling. In the opening set, Hou Yuzhu hit two miraculous serves after deuce at 14 to

A new Chinese spiker in the fierce Olympic final with the Russians in Athens

win 16:14. The loss of the first set put the U.S. team into a state of confusion. The Chinese team took advantage of its opening success to win the whole game in three straight sets. The Chinese team not only won the Olympic gold medal, but also fulfilled its great mission of winning "three consecutive world championships."

The return of the Soviet women's team to the Seoul Games in 1988 made it very difficult for the Chinese team. Although the Chinese girls won the group matches, they lost to the Soviet Union 0:3 in a semifinal. Ultimately, they beat Japan to capture the bronze medal. From then on, the Chinese women's volleyball team began to decline. At the Olympic Games in Barcelona in 1992, China finished in 7th place.

The new rise of the Chinese women's team started when Lang Ping, the "iron hammer" spiker of the former champion team, became its head coach in 1995. She raised the hopes of the team about rising again. Although she helped the team to take the 5th place in the World Cup and the 4th place in the Grand Prix, it was not enough for the team to return to its former glory. Though when the Cuban and Brazilian teams were at their best, the Russian and American teams came back strongly, and the South Korean and Japanese teams were casting eager eyes on the top places, the momentum of the revival and the mental outlook displayed by the Chinese team gave the girls high hopes for their participation in the Atlanta Games. As they had expected, the Chinese team won all three matches in the group series to become one of the eight best teams in the new Olympic tournament. Again, in a quarter-final, the girls beat the German team 3:0 to meet the ambitious Russians in a semi-final. Being fully prepared, the Chinese girls went on to outplay their Russian counterparts 3:1 with a strong defense and fast and varied attacking tactics. In the final, they regrettably lost to the Cuban girls 1:3, but they did show their good form.

After suffering defeats at the Sydney Games, Chen Zhonghe, the team's assistant coach, took over the position of head coach, although not without doubts from critics. He boldly reshuffled the team. All that he did caught the national attention. In a short time, he led the girls to win the World Grand Champions Cup and the World Grand Prix. What is particularly worthy of mention is the fact that he led the girls to win 11 matches in the World Cup to recapture its title after 17 years. The women's volleyball final at the Athens Games was held in the Peace & Friendship Stadium. After two and a half hours of fierce battle, the Chinese team defeated the Russian girls 3:2 in a thrilling match after losing the first two sets. This brought China's gold total to 31 at the Olympics while also winning China's second Olympic volleyball gold medal. The team climbed the Olympic peak once again in 20 years.

■Han Xiaopeng — Feeling as though He Were in a Dream

(Gold medal winner in the aerials of the men's freestyle skiing at the 20th
Olympic Winter Games in Turin, Italy)

Han Xiaopeng, a young Chinese winter Olympian, watched the scene with tears, as though he were in a dream, as the elated Chinese were cheering for joy with fluttering five-starred red flags on a white snow-covered slope under the night sky of the quiet Alps. He won a gold medal in the men's aerials of the freestyle skiing competition at the Turin Winter Olympics in 2006. It was the first gold medal won for China in this Olympic event, thus opening a new chapter in Chinese Olympic skiing history.

He placed first in the preliminary round, but he had no extravagant hopes for a gold medal, because the coach had told him that his stronger rivals usually reserved their best feats for the finals, and that he would have his mission fulfilled if he could finish within the first six places.

The coach designed his strategy with meticulous care: the degree of difficulty for his first jump was 4.425, but it was lowered to 4.175 for his second jump. However, the degree of difficulty was 4.425 for both jumps of his main rival, an athlete from Belarus. The DDs for five of the 12 finalists were bigger than Han's, and one of the DDs was even as high as 4.9. It was beyond Han's capability. In order to avoid interference and enable him to perform in good form, the coach kept reducing the pressure on him so that he could execute the program without any psychological pressure.

The 23-year-old Chinese athlete performed two perfect jumps and received a high score of 250.77 points. The athlete from Belarus had a minor fault in the landing after his second jump. The score for the Belarussian had not yet been announced, but Han thought that he had won the gold. So he began waving the national flag, and jumping with joy.

By this time, the Chinese knew that his dream of winning a gold medal had become a beautiful reality. After the performance, he told the people around him: "It was just like the rough sea within my heart before he landed, but I knew after his landing that the gold medal would be mine." As a matter of fact, Han could also have executed the same difficult move of the last jump as perfectly as the Belarussian did, but in the course of the competition, the Chinese team found that most of the judges refused to give high marks for the difficult move, and therefore changed their tactics instantly, asking Han to execute another move with the degree of difficulty being 4.175 and thus ensuring Han's ultimate victory.

Born in Peixian County, Jiangsu Province, 1982, Han was admitted into the Shenyang Physical Culture Institute as a member of the freestyle skiing team in 1995. He has good physical qualities, and in particular his strength and explosive power were most outstanding among his teammates in the same event. His initial success came very quickly. He won a gold medal at the 1988 National Championships. When he made his Olympic debut in Salt Lake City in 2002, he ranked only 24th, for he had broken the cross ligament of his right knee in training. He was not at all disappointed at his performance, but rather, the poor performance increased his confidence and fighting spirit.

Han Xiaopeng holding up a national flag after winning the gold medal in the men's aerials of the freestyle skiing at the 2006 Olympic Winter Games in Turin, Italy

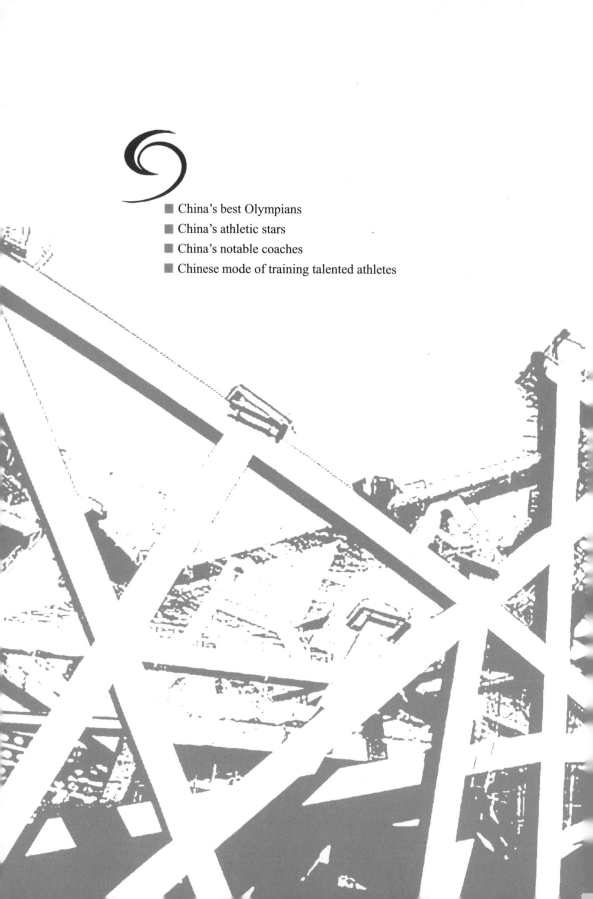

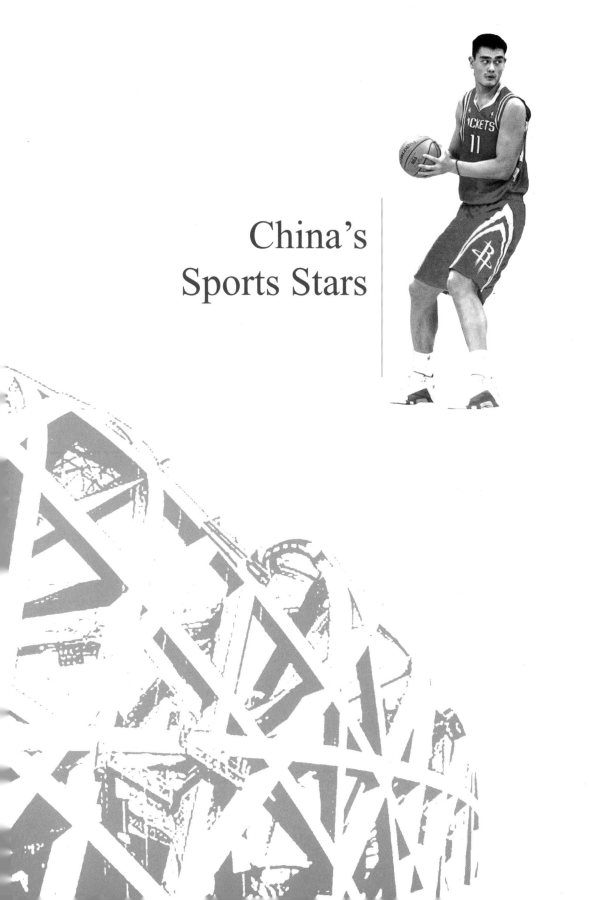

China's
Sports Stars

China's best Olympians

Since Liu Changchun participated in the 10th Olympic Games in 1932, China has produced numerous outstanding athletes and coaches. It is precisely these athletes and coaches who have made China shine brilliantly at the Olympic Games. Their names shall be never forgotten.

■ Yang Chuan-kuang — the Chinese Athlete Who Won China's First Olympic Medal

Yang Chuan-kuang, a decathlete from Chinese Taipei, won a silver medal in 1960 at the 17th Olympic Games in Rome. He was the first Chinese athlete to win an Olympic medal. He was also the only Asian to win an Olympic medal in the track and field events at the 17th Olympic Games, hence his nickname "Asia's iron man."

■ Xu Haifeng — the Chinese Athlete Who Won China's First Olympic Gold Medal

Chinese shooter Xu Haifeng scored 566 points to beat all his rivals in the men's slow-fire free pistol 3×20 event to win the first gold medal of the 23rd Olympic Games in Los Angeles in 1984. He was also the winner of the first gold medal in Chinese Olympic history, ending the era of China's "zero Olympic gold record." In the 88 years prior to the second Los Angeles Olympics, none of the 2,500 gold medals had been awarded to a Chinese athlete.

■Chinese Women's Volleyball Team — the First Chinese Team to Win an Olympic Gold Medal

After losing to the U.S. team in a group match, the Chinese women's volleyball team beat the American rival in the final 3:0 at the Los Angeles Olympic Games in 1984, not only winning an Olympic gold medal, but also fulfilling their dream of "winning the third consecutive top place in the world competions." At the same time, the Chinese women's volleyball team became the first team gold medal winner in Chinese Olympic

The girls of the Chinese women's volleyball team after winning the second
Olympic gold medal in 20 years in the finals at the Athens Games

ATH.

ATHENS 2004

history. Twenty years later, the Chinese women's volleyball team won its second gold medal at the 2004 Olympic Games in Athens.

■Wu Xiaoxuan — China's First Female Olympic Champion

Wu Xiaoxuan won a gold medal in the women's small-bore standard rifle 3×20 and finished third in the air rifle event at the 23rd Olympic Games in Los Angeles in 1984 to become China's first female Olympic champion.

■Chi Cheng — China's First Female Athlete to Win an Olympic Medal

Chi Cheng, a girl from Chinese Taipei, finished her 80m hurdle race in 10.4 seconds to take a bronze medal at the 19th Olympic Games in Mexico in 1968. Although it was a bronze medal, Chi Cheng was the first Asian athlete winning an Olympic medal since the women's track and field events were first added to the Amsterdam Olympic Games in 1928, and the first Chinese woman to win an Olympic medal in Olympic history.

■Chen Jing — China's First Olympic Table Tennis Champion

China's female table tennis player Chen Jing won a gold medal in the women's singles at the 1988 Olympic Games in Seoul to become the first champion in Chinese Olympic history.

■Luan Jujie — Chinese First Olympic Fencing Champion

Luan Jujie won a gold medal in the women's foil event at the 23rd Olympic Games in Los Angeles in 1984 to become China's first Olympic fencing champion. She was also the first Asian fencer to mount the Olympic medal-awarding podium which had previously been dominated by European and American fencers.

■Zeng Guoqiang — China's First Olympic Weightlifting Champion

Zeng Guoqiang from Guangdong Province won a gold medal in the 52kg weight division event at the 23rd Olympic Games in Los Angeles in 1984 to become China's first Olympic weightlifting champion.

■Zhou Jihong — China's First Olympic Diving Champion

Zhou Jihong, an unknown Chinese girl, unexpectedly won a gold medal in the women's platform event at the 23rd Olympic Games in Los Angeles in 1984 to become China's first Olympic diving champion. Since then, diving has become the only sport that has brought gold medals to China at every Olympic Games since China began to participate in the Olympic Games.

Zhou Jihong, Olympic diving champion at the Los Angeles Games and active coach of the Chinese diving team

■**Li Yuwei — Youngest Gold Medalist in Men's 50m Running Target**

Li Yuwei, then aged 19, won gold for China in the men's 50m running target event at the 23rd Olympic Games in Los Angeles. He became the youngest gold medalist in this event in Olympic history.

■Ma Yanhong — China's First Olympic Gymnastic Champion

Ma Yanhong, Chinese women's uneven bars specialist, earned a perfect 10 for her flawless routine performed on the bars at the 1984 Olympic Games in Los Angeles after combating acute stomach pain to become China's first Olympic gymnastic champion.

■Zhuang Xiaoyan — China's First Olympic Judo Champion

Zhuang Xiaoyan defeated five rivals in the women's over-72kg weight division judo event at the 25th Olympic Games in Barcelona in 1992 to win a gold medal. She was the only judo gold medal winner with five straight victories at the Barcelona Games and China's first Olympic judo champion.

Olympic judo champion Zhuang Xiaoyan attending an activity related to the Olympic Games

■Zhuang Yong — China's First Olympic Swimming Champion

Zhuang Yong from Shanghai, 20 years old, won a gold medal in the women's 100m freestyle event at the 25th Olympic Games in Barcelona in 1992. This was not only China's first Olympic gold medal won at the Barcelona Games, but also the first Olympic gold medal ever won in Chinese swimming history.

■Ge Fei/Gu Jun — China's First Olympic Badminton Champions

Ge Fei and Gu Jun, who had been pairing up to play doubles for over ten years and who had won gold medals many times in world competitions, teamed up again to win the doubles final in two straight sets with the same score of 15:5 at the Atlanta Olympic Games in 1996, thus becoming the first Chinese Olympic badminton champions.

■Deng Yaping — the Chinese Athlete Who Has Won the Greatest Number of Olympic Gold Medals for China

Deng Yaping captured four gold medals in the women's singles and doubles at the 25th Olympic Games in 1992 and at the 26th Olympic Games in 1996 to become the athlete with the greatest number of Olympic gold medals in Chinese Olympic history. She paired with Qiao Hong in the doubles at both Olympic Games.

Olympic table tennis champion Deng Yaping taking part in the relay of Athens' Olympic torch in Beijing in 2004

■Li Ning — the Athlete Who Has Won the Greatest Number of Olympic Medals for China

Li Ning won a total of six Olympic medals at the Los Angeles Olympic Games in 1984, including three golds, two silvers and one bronze, to become the Chinese athlete to win the greatest number of Olympic medals. He was also the first Chinese athlete to win three gold medals at the same Olympic Games.

■Wang Yifu — the Chinese Athlete Who Has Participated in the Greatest Number of Olympic Games

Wang Yifu participated in six Olympic Games. At the Olympic Games in Los Angeles in 1984, when Xu Haifeng won the first Olympic gold medal for China, Wang took a bronze medal in the same event. He returned home empty-handed from the Seoul Games in 1988. Wang won his first Olympic gold medal at the 1992 Olympics in Barcelona. He won silver medals at the Atlanta and Sydney Olympic Games in 1996 and 2000. In 2004, Wang won another gold medal in Athens in the men's 10m air pistol event.

■Wang Junxia — the Chinese Athlete Who Has Won Two Olympic Medals in the Track Events

Wang Junxia won a gold medal in the women's 5,000m race and a silver medal in the women's 10,000m race at the Atlanta Olympic Games on July 28, 1996 to become China's first athlete to win two medals in the track events at the same Olympic Games.

■Zhang Shan — a Female Olympic Champion Who Defeated Her Male Rivals

In the mixed doubles trap event at the Barcelona Olympic Games in 1992, Zhang Shan defeated all her male opponents in both the qualifications and the finals with perfect scores to win the gold medal. Not long afterwards, the International Olympic Committee decided to remove this event from the Olympic Program. Although the event was readmitted after 1997, the IOC decided to have the men and women compete in separate events. So, Zhang Shan has become the only female shooter in Olympic history to have defeated all her male rivals to win a gold medal.

■Lou Yun — the First Chinese Athlete Who Defended His Olympic Championship

Lou Yun won gold medals in the men's vaulting horse at the 23rd Olympic Games in Los Angeles in 1984 and the 24th Olympic Games in Seoul in 1988 to become the first Chinese athlete in Chinese Olympic history to defend his Olympic Championship.

■Gao Min — the First Chinese Female Athlete Who Defended Her Olympic Championship

Gao Min twice won the women's springboard diving event, first at the 24th Olympic Games in Seoul in 1988 and then at the 25th Olympic Games in Barcelona in 1992 to become the first Chinese female athlete to defend her Olympic Championship in Chinese Olympic history.

■Fu Mingxia — the Youngest Champion in Olympic History

Fu Mingxia was only 14 years old when she won the platform gold medal at the Barcelona Olympic Games in 1992. She was the youngest champion in Olympic history. At the Atlanta Olympic Games in 1996, Fu took both gold medals in the platform and springboard events, thus becoming the second athlete after Gao Min to defend her Olympic championship in the platform event. This is also a world record. Fu won her second Olympic gold in the springboard event at the 27th Olympic Games in Sydney in 2000.

Fu Mingxia, who won gold medals at three Olympic Games

■Zhu Jianhua — the First Chinese Athlete to Win an Olympic Medal in the Track Event

After breaking the men's world high jump record with a jump of 2.39 meters for the third time just one month earlier, Zhu lost his form and cleared only 2.31 meters at the Los Angeles Olympic Games in 1984 to take a bronze medal. However, he still won the first track and field medal in Olympic history for the People's Republic of China.

■Chen Jingkai — the First Chinese Athlete to Receive an Olympic Silver Order

Chen Jingkai, a pioneer in sports in China, was a famous weightlifter in the 1950s and 1960s. He broke world records on 10 occasions from 1956 to 1964, and was the first

Chinese athlete to break world records. The International Olympic Committee awarded him a silver Olympic Order in recognition of his life-long dedication to the popularization of the Olympic Movement in China. He was the first Chinese athlete to ever receive this honor.

■ Yang Yang — the First Chinese Winner of a Winter Olympic Gold Medal

At the 19th Winter Olympics held in Salt Lake City in 2002, Yang Yang snatched two gold medals in women's 500m and 1,000m speed skating, also the first gold medals China had ever won in Winter Olympic events.

■ Han Xiaopeng — the First Chinese Male Athlete to Win an Olympic Gold Medal in Winter Sports

Han Xiaopeng won a gold medal in the men's aerials of the freestyle skiing competition at the Turin Olympic Winter Games in 2006 to become the first Chinese athlete to win an Olympic gold medal in the men's skiing events.

Yang Yang, an Olympic champion in the short track competition

China's athletic stars |

■Lang Ping — China's Iron Lady

Lang Ping was a leading player when the Chinese women's volleyball team was at its peak. She took part in four major world tournaments from 1981 to 1985 and made a substantial contribution to the team's four consecutive victories. At the 23rd Olympic Games in 1984, she helped the team win its first Olympic gold medal.

In response to a request from the team, Lang Ping, who resided in the United States at the time, came back to Beijing from February 1995 to March 1999 to be its head coach when the team was going through a difficult time.

Lang Ping became the head coach of the U.S. women's volleyball team in 2006.

Lang Ping was in high spirits on her way to watch the opening ceremony of the Athens Olympic Games in 2004

During her four years of coaching, she led the team to take a silver medal at the 1996 Olympic Games in Atlanta, to win the 1997 Asian Championships and to win another silver medal at the 1998 World Championships. In October 2002, she was inducted into the Hall of Fame to become the first Asian volleyball player to receive such an honor.

■Yao Ming — Chinese Star Now Playing for the NBA

Nicknamed "small giant," Yao Ming, 2.26 meters tall, is the pillar of the Chinese men's basketball team. He was chosen by the Houston Rockets in 2002, and was selected as a member of the NBA all-star team for two consecutive seasons.

Yao Ming was born in Shanghai on September 12, 1980. His parents used to be basketball players. Yao Zhiyuan, his father, is 2.08 meters tall and was once a member of the Shanghai men's basketball team while his mother Fang Fengti, 1.88 meters tall, was once a leading member of the Chinese women's basketball player. Born into a family of basketball players, Yao Ming started regular basketball training at a local sports school at the age of nine. Influenced by his parents, Yao Ming soon began to show his understanding of basketball in school.

Yao Ming, basketball star now playing for the NBA's Houston Rockets, wears the No. 11 team shirt.

Yao Ming wears the No. 13 team shirt as a member of the Chinese national team.

Five years later, he became a member of the Shanghai municipal junior basketball team. At 17, he became a member of the Chinese national junior team, and began to wear the national team uniform a year later.

After being selected for the national team, Yao demonstrated a further degree of maturity. During the 2000 Olympic Games, Yao scored an average of 10.5 points, the team's highest score with six rebounds, and 2.2 blocks at every match. His average rate of goals at every match was 63.9 percent, something which no other players could match. At the 2001 Asian Basketball Championships, Yao scored an average of 13.4 points. 10.1 rebounds and 2.8 blocks at every match, and his average rate of goals was 72.4 percent. He helped the Chinese team win the gold medal.

At the NBA draft meeting on June 26, 2002, Yao Ming was chosen by the Houston Rockets to become the first foreign "top draftee" in NBA history.

In his first NBA season, Yao Ming in the No. 11 Rockets team shirt was selected to be a member of the starting line-up of the NBA's all-star team to become the first Asian player given such an honor. In 2003, he became the West's starting center in the all-star match, and received 1,286,324 votes among all star players for the 4th place. In 2004, Yao Ming was again the West's starting center in the all-star match. In the 2005-2006 season, Yao became top scorer among all NBA's star centers with an average of 22 points and 10.3 rebounds.

Yao Ming is an amiable man who is very obliging to other people. He lives a simple life in Houston in a home by a lake with quiet and beautiful surroundings. It is not a very big home, but it has its own features. He likes to stay in his own room where he can see the tiny ripples on the lake through his glass window.

Yao Ming is enthusiastic about public welfare activities.

Yao Ming plays for the Houston Rockets and wears the No. 11 team shirt as a big star in the NBA.

■Ding Junhui — Snooker Prodigy

Prodigy Ding Junhui has been described in the British press as the "Star of the East." He is an introvert, but is eager to put his best foot forward. He is a boy who is soft on the outside but tough on the inside. He began to play billiards at the age of eight, and took third place at an Asian invitational contest when he was 13 years old, hence the nickname of "snooker prodigy."

In May 2002, the 15-year-old boy won his first gold medal for China at the Asian Billiards Championships to become Asia's youngest champion. On August 31 the same year, he won the World Junior Billiards (Snooker) Championship to become China's first world billiard champion. At the Asian Games in October, he defeated a Thai player 3:1 to win the snooker singles gold medal, thus putting an end to China's history of winning no billiard gold medal at the Asian Games. He also joined his teammate to become the team runner-up in the billiards event at the Asian Games. He ranked third at the World Billiards Championships held in Egypt from October 20 through November 2, 2002 to equal China's veteran player Guo Hua's bronze medal record in 1997. On December 15, 2002, the Chinese Billiards Association conferred on Ding the "Chinese Billiard Special Contribution Trophy."

Ding Junhui defeated Mark Williams, who ranked No. 1 in the world at the time,

Ding Junhui playing with full concentration

twice in the Hong Kong and Bangkok legs of the Euro-Asian Masters' Series in August 2003. He became a professional in September 2003. In February 2004, the magnificent moments of Ding defeating Joe Perry, who had a world ranking of No. 16, 6:3 to qualify as one of the 16 best players of the Wembley Masters helped British TV viewers to get to know and take a liking of the billiards boy from the East overnight. In early 2005, Ding played at the Wembley Masters to become one of the eight best players. In April, he defeated Peter Ebdon, Marco Fu, Ken Doherty, and Stephen Hendry at the China Open of the International Billiards & Snooker Federation Ranking Series to win the top place. In December, Ding Junhui again beat all the high-ranking players at the English Championships to win the title.

Ding Junhui defeated Steve Davis, six-time world champion, in the final match at the English Snooker Championships in 2005 to take the trophy.

The significance of Ding's success lies not only in the fact that he has changed the face of Chinese billiards. His development and training methods have evoked wide discussion, and have even aroused debate about the mode of sports training for talented athletes. Ding's development is different from that of most of the other Chinese athletes who have been trained in the traditional pattern of "spare-time sports school — sports school — provincial sports training team — national team." Ding was sent abroad by his father with his own financial resources. His road to success has been stamped with his personal brand, and is now called the "Ding Junhui pattern."

■Zhuang Yong — Golden Swimming Flower

Zhuang Yong is a famous Chinese female swimmer, and one of the "Five Golden Flowers" in Chinese swimming. She took a silver medal in the women's 100m freestyle at the 24th Olympic Games in Seoul in 1988 with a time of 55.47 seconds, the best Asian record in the event. Her success put an end to the record of Chinese swimmers having won no medals at the Olympics. She then went on to win China's first Olympic gold swimming medal in the 100m freestyle at the 25th Games in Barcelona in 1992.

Zhuang Yong was born in Shanghai on August 10, 1972. Her build was good for swimming. When she was five years old, Zhuang Yong, who was still in kindergarten, was spotted by Xu Renhui, a coach from the spare-time sports school in Luwan District, Shanghai. This was the beginning of her contact with water. At the age of seven, she was admitted into the Luwan District Sports School so that she could receive regular training. In 1984, she was selected to the Shanghai municipal swimming team, and then became a member of the national swimming team in 1986. She took second place in the 100m freestyle at the Seoul Olympic Games in 1988 to win the first Olympic swimming medal for China. At the 11th Asian Games in 1900, she won the gold medals in women's 100m freestyle, 200m freestyle, 4×100m freestyle relay and 4×100m medley. She took the gold medals in the women's 50m freestyle and 100m freestyle at the World Swimming Championships in 1991, and won the gold medal in the women's 100m freestyle at the 25th Olympic Games in Barcelona in 1992, China's first Olympic gold medal in swimming. In addition, she won silver medals in the women's 50m freestyle and 4×100m freestyle relay. After the 7th National Games in 1993, she announced her retirement.

Since her retirement, Zhuang Yong often takes part in charity activities.

■Wang Tao — a Happy Table Tennis Expert

There are many stars among the Chinese male table tennis players. Wang Tao is the player who is favored by all for his honesty, discretion and attractiveness.

He was born into a family of musicians. His family has five members. His father and elder brother are violinists. He also began to learn to play the violin in childhood, but in his own words, he stopped playing the violin because of his short fingers. He took to table tennis by chance, and quickly beat all his family members. Consequently, his father sent him to a sports school to learn to play table tennis.

As a player, he has been successful. In his career, he won a gold medal in the mixed doubles and a silver medal in the men's doubles at the 41st World Championships, took both gold medals in the men's doubles and mixed doubles at the 42nd World Championships, and received three gold medals in the men's team event, men's doubles and mixed doubles at the 43rd World Championships. He also captured a gold medal in the mixed doubles at the 25th Olympic Games, a silver medal in the men's singles at the 13th World Cup, became the winner of the grand final of the World Star Tour in 1994, and took two silver medals in the men's singles and men's doubles at the 26th Olympic Games in Atlanta.

Using a bat with a reversed rubber surface for forehand strokes and a natural rubber surface for backhand strokes, the left-handed tennis player resorted to his special tactic of combining a fast attack with loop drives, a unique style adopted for better cooperation with his teammate in the men's doubles, which made him well known in the ping pong world very early. His performances in the men's singles also improved quickly, but were not as good as in the doubles. Wang Tao was best known for his fast backhand flicks in world table tennis. He raised his skills in playing loop drives to new heights and was good at using his power to attack the weaknesses of his opponents. He was a typical player using his brain to play table tennis.

Wang Tao is now the head coach of the August First (the Army) table tennis team with nearly 100 players under his command. Speaking of the future, he has said that while working in the table tennis circle, he must concentrate on it in the hope of training more outstanding players so that Chinese table tennis will have an inexhaustible source of such players.

Wang Tao, a happy table tennis expert

■Deng Yaping — the Greatest Woman Player in the History of Table Tennis

Deng Yaping is the greatest woman player in the history of table tennis. She began to learn to play ping pong with her father. After becoming a member of the Chinese national team in 1988, she won 14 world champion titles, and remained No. 1 in the world in table tennis for eight consecutive years. She is the only table tennis championship defender at the Olympic Games with four gold medals in the bag, two in the singles and two in the doubles with her partner Qiao Hong.

During her training sessions, the instructions she received most often from her coach were not "what you should do", but "have more rest, don't outdo yourself." Someone on the team kept a record for her: she practiced for an average of 40 extra minutes every day. In other words, she practiced 40 days more than other players. In fact, her amount of training greatly exceeded that of a normal player. Zhang Xielin, a long-time head coach for the women players in the national team, recalled that Deng had two pairs of shoes for her training sessions. If the shoes she wore became wet, she would put on another pair. A basket has more than 200 balls for training, and she would use more than 10 baskets. The movement of her feet in practicing a group of strokes amounted to a 400m run. A training session for Deng amounted to a 10,000m race. This did not include the thousands of movements required to swing her bat.

Her hard work in training was finally rewarded. She was admitted to the national team in November 1988. Five months later, the 16-year-old girl won her first world title in the women's doubles at the 40th World Table Tennis Championships.

The fierce battle between China and South Korea in the women's team event at the 11th Asian Games in Beijing in 1990 is the best memory that the Chinese people have of Deng Yaping. In the finals, the 17-year-old became the favorite star of the spectators for her unique mettle displayed in competition while she appeared as the leading player of the women's team.

Deng reached her peak at the Barcelona Olympic Games in 1992 as far as her age and performance were concerned. Being the absolute key player of the Chinese team, she won both gold medals in the singles and doubles without any difficulty. Again at the Atlanta Olympics in 1996, she took both gold medals to defend her championship position. Joan Samaranch, then IOC President, watched her match and personally awarded her gold medal.

She dominated all major international tournaments in the women's singles and

Deng Yaping is one of China's greatest table tennis players in the Chinese history of table tennis.

doubles before her retirement in the late 1990s, a period which was acclaimed in the Chinese press as "Deng's Era."

■Zhang Shan — a Woman Who Does Not Yield to Men

Born in 1968, Zhang Shan was enrolled in a children's sports school during her childhood. At the beginning, she learned to play basketball. When she was 16 and half years old, she began to use a gun, and her performance was outstanding. In 1984, she became a member of the Sichuan provincial shooting team and was selected for the national team for intensive training in 1989.

Zhang Shan scored 200 hits out of 200 shots in the qualifying round of the double trap event at the Barcelona Olympic Games in 1992, turning the term "100 percent accuracy" into reality. Then, she won the gold medal. Her gold medal carried special weight, because double trap was a mixed event open to both sexes. Zhang Shan thus became the first woman shooter to win the double trap gold medal in Olympic history and the sole woman with such an honor in history, as double trap was divided into two separate events at subsequent Games. She not only performed the miracle of a woman shooter giving no way to the male shooters, but also became the first Chinese woman to break the European monopoly on this event.

The 1992 Olympic Games marked the first summit she climbed in her career. However, just at the peak of her career, the event was removed from the Olympic program by the International Olympic Committee. It was not until 1997, five years later, that the event was readmitted. Zhang Shan also came back and captured the gold medal at the World Cup in Cairo in 1998, thus taking an extra ticket for the Chinese shooting team's entry in the 2000 Olympic Games in Sydney.

Zhang Shan is a typical girl born in Sichuan Province. She is honest, sincere, resolute, independent, and straightforward. When in competition, she fired every shot resolutely and accurately. When asked what would make her the happiest, she said frankly: taking a gold medal is not what would make me the happiest. Getting married is what would make me the most happy.

■Liu Xuan — the Youngest Late Bloomer

Liu Xuan began gymnastic training when she was studying in primary school in Jixiang Lane, Changsha City, Hunan Province in 1984. She received regular training in the Hunan provincial gymnastic team at the age of eight, and became a member of the national team at 13. She was one of the leading gymnasts in the

Liu Xuan's graceful posture in gymnastic competition

1990s when the Chinese women's gymnastic team was previously at its highest point. She served on the national team for many years and fought side by side with Mo Huilan, Zhou Duan, Qiao Ya, Ye Linlin, Ji Liya, Bi Wenjing, Meng Fei and Kui Yuanyuan, thus creating a record of being the oldest gymnast in the Chinese women's gymnastic team.

Liu Xuan made her debut at the 1994 Asian Games in Hiroshima, Japan, and joined

Liu Xuan standing on the podium after receiving her Olympic gold medal in Sydney

the other members of her team in taking the team gold medal and a silver medal in the uneven bars.

On the young Chinese women's gymnastic team, Liu was a late bloomer. She appeared at two Olympic Games, two Asian Games and three World Championships between 1994 and 2000. It was not until 1998 that she won her first world championship title at the World Cup. Two years later, she won her first Olympic gold medal on the balance beam at the Sydney Games.

Liu is gentle and quiet, but at the same time, she is also a vivacious girl. In her training, she was good at using her brain. Her movements were harmonious, and she had good power and flexibility. She had originally prepared a very difficult exercise called "single-arm circle with Zinkel somersault," but it was not recognized by the International Gymnastics Federation on the grounds that the "exercise is not suitable for the physical growth of women gymnasts." Liu's rich degree of experience was also a great help to her younger teammates. In competition, she was always the first to appear on the podium, because she was always calm in executing exercises and helping her teammates to keep calm during their performances.

Having completed her studies at Peking University, Liu has tried many new things, including posing for advertisements, anchoring a newscast and being a mistress of ceremonies. Her new goal is to be a gymnastic judge at the Beijing Olympic Games in 2008.

■Sang Lan — the Most Dependable and Most Beautiful Girl

Many people still remember that a beautiful small girl fell heavily onto the floor due to a faulty move in the vaulting horse competition at the 4th Goodwill Games in New York, July 1998. She is Sang Lan, a member of the Chinese women's gymnastics team. Her cervical spinal cord was severely injured and her body was completely paralyzed below the chest.

A lively and cheerful girl, Sang Lan was the vaulting champion at the 7th National Games. Before her injury, her skills had been improving steadily. She was very likely to become another shining star of the Chinese women's gymnastic team. However, unexpected misfortune befell the 17-year-old girl.

After the injury, she did not give up. Her optimistic mood won her admiration from all the people who knew her. She started her college education at Peking University in 2002, majoring in journalism at the Department of Journalistic and Communication Studies. Since then, she has become a TV anchorwoman. If gymnastics was once the most important part of her life, she now has a broader vision as a TV sports journalist. She has to know about other sports. Apart from gymnastics, she also likes volleyball, badminton and rhythmical gymnastics. What she loves are the graceful and lively sports, although she now has to sit in her wheelchair to do everything.

Life has placed her many difficulties in her path, but she has overcome them. Today, she not only has her own program, but also takes part in various activities with great devotion. Since being away from the competitive arena, her positive mental state is sufficient to get her a position in any line of work in which she would like to take part.

Sang Lan taking part in the relay of the Athens Olympic torch

China's notable coaches |

■Ma Yuehan — (track and field coach)

Born in Xiamen City in Fujian Province, Ma Yuehan graduated from St. Johns University in Shanghai in 1911. While at school, he was a leading member of the school's football, tennis, baseball, and track and field teams. Being good at middle and long distance races, he won both the 880 yard and 440 yard races of the schools' united teams at the First National Games in 1910. Ma went to the United States twice from 1919 to 1926 for advanced study in physical culture. He was the head coach of the track and field team of the Chinese delegation to the 11th Olympic Games in Berlin in 1936. He was an assistant teacher, professor and

The statue of Ma Yuehan in his hometown Xiamen

director of the Department of Physical Culture at Tsinghua University from 1914 to 1966. During his 52 years of physical education, he studied the laws of sports, and worked out nearly 100 sets of free-standing exercises with different contents and had his writings published, including *The Value of the Changes of Sports* and *Our Due Understanding of Physical Education*. Ma dedicated his life to the promotion of physical education and gave enthusiastic guidance to young people in doing physical exercises. He was an exemplary teacher and enjoyed moral eminence and high esteem. Ma was highly regarded by the government and earned the respect of the people. For years after 1954, he was the president of the Chinese Track and Field Association, and vice president and later president of the All-China Sports Federation.

■Mao Dezhen (track and field coach)

Born in Dalian City, Mao Dezhen was a long-distance runner on the national track and field team in the late 1950s, and became a coach in the city's spare-time sports school after he retired from active service on the team. He was the trainer of Mu Weiguo and Sun Ripeng and other outstanding athletes. In 1995, he became the coach for Wang Junxia, holder of the world records in the women's 3,000m and 10,000m races. Thanks to his effective coaching, Wang Junxia won the gold medal in the 5,000m race and the silver medal in the 10,000m race at the 26th Olympic Games in Atlanta in 1996.

■Huang Yubin (gymnastics coach)

Huang Yubin became a member of the Heilongjiang provincial gymnastic team in 1970, and then a member of the national team in 1975. He is an all-round gymnast, good at all apparatus, but still his best apparatus is the rings. Huang is the first Chinese male gymnast to perform the whole set of movements with arms extended at the rings.

Huang won the gold medal in

Huang Yubin and members of his team after their return from Athens

the rings at the 8th Asian Games in 1978, took sixth place in the rings at the 20th World Gymnastics Championships in 1979, shared the first place in the rings with Soviet gymnast Makuts and took the third place at the 1980 World Cup Gymnastics Tournament. In 1981, he was runner-up in the rings and took the third place with other teammates in the team event at the 21st World Gymnastics Championships. He was one of the leading members of the Chinese team capturing the men's team gold medal and taking a bronze medal in the rings at the 9th Asian Games in 1982.

After 1985, Huang has been a coach of the national team and its deputy head coach after 1992. He was promoted to the position of head coach in 1997. The world champions under his coaching include Fan Di, Li Jing, Li Chunyang, Li Xiaoshuang, and Huang Liping.

■Cai Zhenhua (table tennis coach)

Popularly known as a "young marshal," Cai Zhenhua is a dramatic person in Chinese table tennis history. He became an assistant coach at 28, the head coach of the men's national team at 30, and head coach of the national team at 35. Since becoming a coach of the Chinese table tennis team, the Goddess of Good Luck has never been far away from him. In June 1989, he was officially assigned to coach the Italian national team. In November 1989, he became the coach of the Chinese men's team and then its head coach in June 1991. He led the Chinese team to take the men's doubles gold medal at the Barcelona Olympic Games in 1992, the men's team title at the 42nd World Table Tennis Championships in 1995, and the gold medals in the men's singles and men's doubles at the Atlanta Olympic Games in 1996. After he took over the post of head coach of the Chinese national team in June 1997, Cai led the team to take part in all major international tournaments with resounding successes: the men's team title at the 44th World Championships in 1997, six titles at the Asian Games in 1998, the first two places at the women's World Cup in 1998, the first two places in four individual events at the ITTF Pro-Tour in 1998, six titles at the 45th World championships in 1999, a clean gold sweep (four events), three silver medals and one bronze at the Sydney Olympic Games, a clean gold sweep (seven events), four silver medals and five bronze medals at the 46th World Championships in 2001, both men's and women's title at the 2002 World Cup, four titles at the 47th World Championships in 2003, the men's World Cup title in 2003, four titles and three second places in the individual events in the year-end finals of the Pro-Tour in 2003, and a clean sweep of the one-two-three at the 8th World Cup in 2003. The Chinese team also took the men's and women's team titles at the Qatar World Championships and three gold medals, one silver medal and three bronze medals at the Athens Olympics in 2004.

Cai Zhenhua and his disciples

Weightlifting coach Chen Wenbin

Chen Wenbin (weightlifting coach)

Since 1996, Chen Wenbin has trained six weightlifters to become world champions. They are Wang Guohua, Wan Jianhui, Shi Zhiyong, Wu Meijin, Zhang Guozheng and Li Hongli. He received certificates of honor in sports issued by the State Sports Administration on five occasions between 1996 and 2002. In 1999, he was named one of China's 10 best coaches.

The three weightlifters he coached — Shi Zhiyong, Zhang Guozheng and Wu Meijin — won two gold medals and one silver at the Athens Olympic Games in 2004, and, as a result, he has been honored as a gold medal coach.

Li Yongbo (badminton coach)

Li Yongbo is one of China's famous badminton players. After becoming a coach, he led the Chinese badminton team to capture the Sudirman Cup five times (1995, 1997, 1999, 2001 and 2005), the Uber Cup five times (1998, 2000, 2002, 2004 and 2006), and the Thomas Cup twice (2004 and 2006).

After Li took over the position from Wang Wenjiao and Chen Fushou as the head coach of the Chinese badminton team in 1993, he completely reshuffled the team, developed a young coaching staff and trained young players. His first success came in 1995, when he led the Chinese badminton team to capture the Sudirman Cup, a mixed team event symbolizing a country's overall strength. His team again won the Sudirman Cup in 1997 and in 1999. The women players won the doubles at the Atlanta Olympic Games in 1996. This was the first Olympic gold medal won by the Chinese badminton team since badminton became an Olympic sport in 1992. At the 1997 World Championships, China won three gold medals, demonstrating that Chinese badminton had again climbed to the top of the world. The Chinese women's team recovered the Uber Cup in 1998 after four years without it, and defended it easily in 2000. The Sydney Olympic Games marked the peak of Li's coaching career as he led the Chinese team to take four gold medals. China dropped to the third place at the 22nd Thomas Cup held in 2002, but it took the Uber Cup for the third consecutive time. In 2003, China lost the Sudirman Cup to South Korea, failing to fulfill its dream of winning the cup five consecutive times. China recovered the cup at the 9th Sudirman Cup held in Beijing in 2005.

Li is known for his resoluteness and strictness in coaching young players. He has paid great attention to the training of a reserve force. The upcoming young players he has trained in all events have become an inexhaustible source of talent enabling the Chinese badminton team to retain its supremacy in the badminton world.

Li Yongbo, head coach of the Chinese badminton team

■Ma Junren (track and field coach)

Ma Junren is a legendary Chinese track and field coach. When he was coach, the Liaoning provincial women's middle and long distance running team won three gold medals in the 1,500m, 3,000m and 10,000m races at the World Track and Field Championships in 1993. At the 7th National Games, his team members broken world records in the 1,500m, 3,000m and 10,000m races one after another, adding the most brilliant chapter to date to the Chinese history of track and field events. He produced a group of world-class middle and long distance runners like Qu Yunxia, Wang Junxia, Dong Yanmei and Jiang Bo. The Liaoning women's middle and long distance running team was once known as "an army unit of Ma's family."

Born in 1944, Ma served under the Liaoning Military Provincial Area Command. He became a coach in the Anshan City's Spare-time Sports School. In 1988, he was employed as a coach for the women's middle and long distance running group under the Liaoning provincial track and field team. He created a set of peculiar training methods; that is, combining training with free oxygen and training without free oxygen, running long distances to develop endurance to improve the stamina for short distances and running short distances to improve the speed and skills to improve performance in the long distance runs.

Ma Junren, a famous long distance running coach

■Xu Yiming (diving coach)

In May 2003, the International Swimming Federation (FINA) held a grand ceremony in the United States to award a prize to Xu Yiming, the former head coach of the Chinese diving team. The International Hall of Fame in Fort Lauderdale added Xu's fingerprints and footprints. He thus became the first Chinese coach to win this honor in the international sports world. For decades, he devoted himself to the sport of diving in China and the world, and made tremendous contribution to the development of the sport with his brilliant accomplishments.

Born in a small town on the Leizhou Peninsula near Zhenjiang in Guangdong Province in 1942, he became an amateur diver at 15. He won his first gold medal in the men's platform event at a national contest in 1972. In the following year, he became a coach of the Chinese diving team. Before long, he had improved the safety belt, ground bouncing net, underwater dust absorber and other training facilities for divers. In order to raise the level of difficulty in training he introduced the half-meter springboard to increase training safety and make the training exercises more scientific. The small boys and girls were forced to dive into the water like ducks and perform dives one after another under his "manipulation." It is precisely at these original safety facilities that the children have avoided the dangers of being injured and been relieved of their worries. The young divers very quickly improved the complexity of their dives to reach the current top world level. For this reason, Xu has received exceptionally good feedback in the diving world.

Xu's name is recorded on every page of the record of merits of the modern Chinese sport of diving. Among the top divers he trained are: Li Kongzheng, bronze medal winner in the men's platform at the 1984 Olympic Games and silver medal winner in the men's platform at the 1986 World Championships; Shi Meiqin, gold medal winner in the women's springboard competition at the 1981 World Cup; Tan Liangde, three-time silver medal winner in the men's springboard competition at the 1984, 1988 and 1992 Olympic Games; Zhou Jihong, gold medal winner in the women's platform event at the 1984 Olympic Games; Chen Lin, gold medal winner in the women's platform event at the 1986 World Championships; Xu Yanmei, gold medal winner in the women's platform event at the 1988 Olympic Games; Gao Min, twice gold medal winner in the women's springboard competition at the 1988 and 1992 Olympic games; Sun Shuwei, gold medal winner in the men's platform event at the 1992 Olympic Games; Fu Mingxia, twice gold medal winner in the women's platform event at the 1992 and 1996 Olympic Games and twice gold medal winner in the women's springboard competition at the 1996 and 2000 Olympic Games; Xiong Ni, gold medal winner in the men's springboard competition at the 1996 and 2000 Olympic Games; and Tian Liang, gold medal winner in the men's platform event at the 2000 Olympic Games.

Chinese mode of training talented athletes |

By the end of 2004, Chinese athletes had won a total of 1,795 Olympic and world champion titles at the Olympic Games and other major world tournaments. They had broken or surpassed world records on 1,119 occasions. In the more than 50 years since the founding of the People's Republic of China in 1949, the country has achieved outstanding results in the competitive sports, making China a strong power in the world of competitive sports, and an important member of the Olympic family. Hard struggle, determination, unity, cooperation and the spirit of striving for national honor displayed in training and competition have become a valuable spiritual asset of the Chinese nation, and have encouraged the Chinese people generation after generation. The brilliant successes in China's sports are largely attributed to the "whole-nation system."

■Whole-nation System

In the past half century, the development of Chinese sports has consistently followed the Soviet training model. All expenses for the training of every professional athlete from childhood on are covered by the nation. The training of an athlete for the national teams requires large financial input. This mode of training athletes for the competitive sports is called the "whole-nation system." Since the beginning of the period of reform, the Chinese whole-nation system of training talented athletes for competitive sports has also changed and improved. It has gradually become a national sports system with Chinese characteristics.

The characteristics of the "whole-nation system" are:

First, youth with athletic potentials are able to receive professional training as early as possible. The early specialized training is mainly conducted in the children's sports schools and sports training centers. The coaching staff of these schools consists of professional coaches who have been educated in the physical education colleges or who have served on national or provincial teams when they were active athletes. In these schools, the time allocated for training is guaranteed, the training content has clear purposes, and the training is conducted strictly according to the training program. Compared with the children of the same age in other countries, the children who have been chosen are often better trained. Especially in the sports with higher technical contents, the rate of successful athletes after training is higher than in other countries.

Second, policies that involve bonuses intended to arouse the enterprising spirit of the young athletes are adopted. In order to encourage local sports departments and grassroots coaches and trainers to train outstanding youth and deliver them to higher training institutions, the State Sports Administration has formulated and issued a series of bonus policies. For example, if an athlete wins a gold medal at a summer or winter Olympics, the gold

In the Chinese national training hall for diving

The China Institute of Sports Science (CISS)
under the State Sports Administration

medal and other medals the athlete wins and the delegation he belongs are both recorded at the national games held in the following year, and the athlete can receive the same bonus as an athlete who wins a gold medal or receive prizes at the national games. The positioning of the delegation on the gold medal tally can also be moved higher. To give another example, if an athlete wins a gold medal or other medal, not only is his current coach awarded, but his first coach is also awarded correspondingly according to

The sports schools in China are the places where the Chinese Olympic champions first receive their training. The photo shows the boys training at a local sports school.

prescribed percentages.

Third, permanent national teams are established. Although there are permanent national teams in many countries today, China's complete national team system is unique. China not only has permanent national teams for the Olympic sports, but it also has permanent national teams for non-Olympic sports which have an important influence, such as *weiqi* (go) and (international) chess. The Training Bureau of the State Sports Administration is a typical example of this approach. It has national teams for a dozen sports, including diving, gymnastics, swimming, table tennis, badminton, weightlifting, basketball and volleyball. As the gold medals for the Chinese Olympic Delegations have been won mostly by the athletes of these teams under the Training

Bureau, it has been called the "base camp" for China's Olympic gold medals in Chinese sports circles. For example, of the 32 gold medals received by the Chinese Olympic delegation at the 28th Olympic Games in Athens, 22 came from the athletes of the teams under the Bureau. The Training Bureau not only has the best coaches in the country, including Huang Yubin, Cai Zhenhua and Li Yongbo, but also has the most up-to-date training facilities available, such as a gymnastics hall, a table tennis hall, a diving hall, basketball and volleyball halls and apartments for athletes. In addition, an institution of sports science and an information institution closely related to the daily training and preparations for major international competitions are both located close to the training halls, and a hospital specializing in illnesses and injuries is found within the compound of the training halls, thus ensuring that the research services and medical services are available whenever they are needed. For example, when the Chinese track and field team was preparing for the Athens Olympic Games, the China Institute of Sports Science assigned 13 researchers to assist with Liu Xiang's training during each of his training sessions. There were three video cameras shooting every movement he executed. The recorded materials were used for analysis and study, and the research results were converted into discs for Liu and his coach. All these conditions were made possible by the government.

It is also undeniable that there are clear shortcomings in the "whole-nation system." Under such a system, the athletes experience only a monotonous form of athletic training from beginning to end, and lack training in multiple skill sets and lack choices for individual development. At the same time, the system also leads to a monotonous system for the evaluation of their achievements at school, in the specialized teams and

Chinese badminton players in a mixed doubles match

national teams. Together with the athletes, they wait for chances to fight for fame at one stroke.

■China's sports professionalism

The "Decision to Broaden Reform in the Realm of Sports," issued in 1992, articulated the goal of establishing a new Chinese-type sports system. Soon afterwards, football became the first sport to adopt professionalism "with sports reform and mechanism change as the core, focusing on turning the football association into an entity, introducing the club system and developing the football industry."

The Marlboro National Football Division A League Series was born in April 1994, marking a new phase of development for China's professional sports. After the initial results were achieved in the reform of professional football, professional league systems were also established for basketball, volleyball, table tennis, badminton and chess.

After 1994, within a short period of time, Chinese sports represented by football became the destination for the concentration of substantial social resources. The concentration of social resources with the spectators' attention as the most essential motivating force turned Chinese sports into a target pursued by the media and capital.

Professionalism has become the platform for sports to take in social resources, and at the same time has built the new system for the accumulation of wealth of athletes. Professionalism is the watershed in time for the accumulation of wealth of the Chinese athletes. This milestone event in the Chinese history of sports development has changed the level of wealth of the Chinese athletes. The athletes have experienced a progression of going from meager pay to enormous income. So, when we review the history of wealth of Chinese athletes, we cannot fail to mention professionalism in sports.

Under China's market economic conditions, sports professionalism may serve as a route to the development of sports and the sports industry. However, even in the economically developed countries, it is impossible for all sports to be highly professionalized. Only a small number of spectator sports which attract large crowds and have talented people capable of managing them can find themselves like fish in the water in the sports market. If professionalism is introduced when conditions are not conducive, there are inevitably many difficulties. It will still take a long time to successfully professionalize sports in China.

- Chinese folk sports
- Development of non-Olympic sports
- Nationwide fitness campaign
- Construction of stadiums and gymnasiums
- The sports industry

China's Sports among the People

Residents in Shenyang, Liaoning Province, taking part in walking along the Olympic Fitness Road

Shuttlecock kicking, a popular
game among the Chinese people

People waving flagpoles as part of a folk game in Beijing's countryside

A dragon boat race in southern China during the Dragon Boat Festival (the fifth day of the fifth month of the lunar calendar)

Horse racing at the winter Nadam Fair in Inner Mongolia

Chinese Folk Sports

Traditional Chinese folk sports have a long history. They were gradually created by the people of various ethnic groups in the course of their lives, and passed on from generation to generation as an important means to improve their fitness and level of relaxation after hard work. Each and every one of their characteristics is linked with Chinese culture, and they fully display the fascinating charm of the Chinese folk culture and customs.

Since wushu (martial arts) was demonstrated at the 11th Olympic Games, the traditional Chinese folk sports have found favor among the sports lovers of all countries，and have received more and more attention in the sports circles. At present, there are dozens of traditional folk sports in China. They all have their own characteristics and styles. This chapter will give brief accounts of some traditional folk sports which have had an important influence on the following pages:

Wushu

Wushu is also known as "guoshu," "martial arts" or "kung fu." It is a sport encompassing combat techniques for attack and defense involving the use of bare hands and weaponry. It includes movements and skills in the form of routines and combat to strengthen

An old man practicing wushu in front of the Baoguo Temple

the body, develop will and determination, and improve combat skills. Wushu has a long history and broad foundation among the people in China. It is part of China's fine cultural heritage.

Wushu developed from the production activities of man in primitive society. Its weaponry originated from the primitive instruments used for production. The simple ideas relating to attack and defense were derived from the struggles against nature. The embryonic form of wushu was related to the wars after the emergence of class and state. By the periods of the Qin and Han dynasties, hand combat and swordsmanship were already very popular. Imperial examinations specializing in military knowledge and skill were introduced in the Tang Dynasty and promoted the military exercises. In the Song Dynasty, there were demonstrations of fighting with fists, kicking, waving broad swords and etc. In the imperial courts, there were "spear and shield" and "sword and shield" practices in pairs. From that period on, wushu was gradually and mainly practiced in routines. Different schools and different styles of wushu were formed one after another and the "skills in wielding the 18 kinds of weapons" and the various schools and styles of quan (boxing) became widespread.

The sport of Chinese wushu is deeply rooted in the fertile soil of Chinese traditional culture and encompasses the depth of Chinese philosophy. It has developed from simple hunting and combat techniques into a traditional Chinese sport with rich Chinese traditional cultural significance that has many functions, stresses exercises to both improve the internal organs and to strengthen the muscles and bones, and puts equal emphasis on skills and techniques.

Wushu contains many traditional forms of strengthening the muscles and bones, such as the Five-Animal Exercise, (an exercise consisting of movements imitating the movements and expressions of tigers, deer, bears, apes and birds), Eight-Duan Jin (an eight-element exercise for improving internal organs, energy and blood), Twelve-Duan Jin (a 12-element exercise for improving internal organs, energy and blood), 22-Stance Muscle-Improving Exercise, 24-Seasonal Division Points Sitting Stances for Health Improvement Diagram, Taiji Exercise for Improving Internal Organs, and Nei Gong Quan (a style of boxing exercise for improving internal organs). Wushu exercises are easy to learn and to do. They require no special venue, and only simple equipment and little investment. Besides,

Spear — a wushu weapon

wushu has many different forms, and can vary from person to person.

Wushu enjoys a great degree of popularity among the Chinese people. At the same time, as more wushu competitions and demonstrations are held abroad, and Chinese kung fu films are shown, wushu is gradually becoming a world sport.

Shuttlecock

Shuttlecock is a folk sport with national characteristics among the Chinese people. According to historical records and archaeological relics which have been unearthed, shuttlecock kicking originated in the Han Dynasty (206 BC-AD220), and began to become popular in the Tang Dynasty (618-907). Shops

Shuttlecock kicking, a popular game in China

making and selling shuttlecocks were found at the fairs. In the Ming Dynasty (1368-1644), there were formal shuttlecock kicking competitions. The sport reached its peak in the Qing Dynasty (1644-1911), and the making and kicking techniques were unprecedented. A grand shuttle kicking demonstration was held outside Di'anmen in Beijing in 1912, and a shuttlecock kicking organization was set up.

The method of making traditional shuttlecocks is as follows: Rooster feathers are tied together and inserted into the square hole of a coin which is then tightly wrapped by cloth and sewn. There are different kinds of shuttlecocks, some made of rooster feathers, some of hair, some of paper strips, and some of woolen threads.

There are essentially four kicking techniques: "kicking with the inner side of the foot, with the leg bent inside; kicking with the outer side of the foot, with the leg bent outside; kicking backward with the heel; and kicking forward with the instep." Competitions are organized on the basis of the kicking technique. The traditional matches include number play, time play and variety play. Shuttlecock kicking is a good exercise for strengthening the whole body. It requires no special venue or equipment. The amount of physical exertion can vary from person to person. It is a good game for people of all age groups for improving flexibility, coordination and fitness.

The first formal Chinese shuttlecock kicking tournament was organized by the Guangzhou Municipal Sports Commission in 1956. Simple rules were formulated. The formal *Competition Rules for Shuttlecock* were published in the country in 1984. They were based on the characteristics of shuttlecock kicking and some of the rules for ball games.

Chinese Chess

Chinese chess is played between two people. It is a chess game in which one side wins a game by "checkmating" or capturing the opponent's general (marshal). There are hundreds of millions of chess players in the country. This game not only enriches the cultural life of the people and refines their sentiments, but also develops intellectual power, improves thinking, increases the ability for dialectical analysis and enhances strength of will.

Chinese chess has a long history. There are historical records of chess being played in the Warring States Period (770-476 BC). Constant changes were made in the shape of the chess pieces during the Three Kingdoms (220-280), and Chinese chess was first introduced into India at that time. During the Sui and Tang dynasties (581-907), we find more historical records about the playing of chess. This can be confirmed by the objects unearthed in archaeological findings. For example, the Suzhou brocades in the early years of the Northern Song Dynasty (960-1127) were decorated with designs of "plucking instruments (music), chess, calligraphy and painting," and chessboards with eight squares by eight squares in chiaroscuro. Bronze chess pieces painted with designs on the reverse side have been unearthed in Kaifeng, Henan Province. Conclusions can be drawn from these objects that the shapes and structure of Chinese chess in the Tang Dynasty were very similar to the early form of the (international) chess. After several hundred years of practice, Chinese chess had its chess pattern finalized in the late years of the Northern Song Dynasty

Yu Youhua, a grand master of Chinese chess, playing chess with 100 children

as modern chess: 32 pieces, a chessboard with a neutral boundary river area, and the General and the Marshal placed in the center of the Palace with nine intersections.

Since 1956, Chinese chess has been considered a national sport in China. In recent years, the men's team event, women's singles event and women's team event have been added to the competition program, in addition to the men's singles. The best players have conferred on them the title of "master" and "grand master" by the State Physical Culture and Sports Commission (predecessor of the State Sports Administration). The Chinese Chess Association was formed in 1962, with corresponding organs throughout the country. Thanks to the mass activities and organized matches, the playing level has risen very fast, and outstanding chess players have emerged one after the other. The well-known players include Yang Guanlin, Hu Ronghua, Liu Dahua, Zhao Guorong, Li Laiqun, Lu Qin and Xu Yinchuan.

above : Chang Hao — a young *weiqi* master
below : Chinese and Japanese players meet
at the chessboard very often.

▊*Weiqi* (go)

Weiqi (go) is the oldest form of chess in human history. Playing weiqi is the product of combining scientific character with artistic quality and an activity of intellectual competition full of wit and interest. Chinese weiqi has a 3,000-year-old history. It was introduced to other East Asian countries 1,000 years ago, and to many countries in Europe and America in past decades.

Weiqi was created in China. Ancient Chinese people regarded playing chess to be a symbol of refinement and elegance. Weiqi thus became the subject of poems and painting by artists and men of letters. Chinese ancient books on weiqi include principles, chess manuals, moves such as attack and defense, dead and alive, taking stock of the situation and making closing moves. They are the crystallization of the painstaking intellectual work of the ancient players in the past centuries and provide valuable data for studying the skills of ancient times. Therefore, they have received universal attention from both inside and outside China.

Weiqi is played with 181 black and 180 white, flat round pieces called stones, on a square board checkered by 19 vertical lines and 19 horizontal lines to form 361 intersections. The equipment is very simple. The game can be played anywhere. In the course of play, a player has to make decisions in a limited timeframe about how to cope with a quickly changing situation. It is not hard to imagine how tense the atmosphere can become. A good move can put one's opponent in an awkward situation, but a wrong move may lead to the loss of a game. Therefore, the game requires both daring and calmness. Playing *weiqi* helps to strengthen one's determination and strength of will, and in general, increases one's ability to make cool-minded judgments.

The exchange of visits between the Chinese and Japanese *weiqi* masters is a great event in the Chinese *weiqi* world. About 1,500 years ago, *weiqi* was introduced into Japan through the Korean Peninsula. Ever since the beginning in the 1960s, the Chinese-Japanese *Weiqi* Challenge Series has become one of the major tournaments in the *weiqi* world.

Chinese wrestling

■ Chinese-style Wrestling

Chinese-style wrestling is a type of bare-handed wrestling played between two individuals.... It is a competitive sport in which the winner is the wrestler who throws his opponent to the ground. It is one of the oldest traditional Chinese sports.

In ancient times, wrestling (*shuaijiao*), was called jiaoli, jiaodi, xiangpu, zhenjiao and shuaijiao, and only came to be called wrestling in modern times. It was originally played by hand-to-hand combat, developed from the bare-handed combat techniques of throwing, striking, kicking and holding. Five thousand years ago, our forefathers started wrestling activities. It was initially practiced for military purpose only, and began to be a mass sport and recreational game in the Qin and Han dynasties (221 BC-AD 220). The royal families had special wrestling organizations which continued

People competing in a dragon boat race

to evolve in the form of shanpuying (charity wrestling battalion) in the Qing Dynasty. In the last three dynasties of Yuan, Ming and Qing (1279-1911), wrestling became a sport of the Manchu and Mongolian peoples, and gradually evolved into the embryonic form of modern Chinese wrestling. In 1953, Chinese wrestling was included in the national competition sports program, and a national contest was organized. After that, national wrestling championships were held annually. The State Physical Culture and Sports Commission issued the *Weight Division System for Chinese Wrestlers* in 1956, and issued the *Chinese Wrestling Regulations* in 1957. These regulations were revised in 1986.

When a Chinese wrestling tournament is organized, the wrestlers are divided into ten weight categories. A match consists of 3 periods of 3 minutes each, with two 1-minute intermissions. The athletes wrestle on an 8×8m mat. They wear special soft, durable wrestling short-sleeved vests, waist belts and long trousers. They are permitted to hold each other and grab each other's waist belts and vests, but not the trousers. The judges award 3, 2 or 1 point to the wrestlers according to the manner in which they have thrown their opponent to the ground. The winner is the wrestler who gets the most aggregated points.

■Dragon Boat

Dragon is the symbol of the Chinese nation. As early as during the Spring and Autumn and the Warring States periods (770-221 BC), people began to paint dragon heads, scales and tails on wooden boats. This was the earliest form of a dragon boat.

The custom of dragon boat racing is said to have started in order to honor the death of the patriotic poet Qu Yuan who drowned himself in a river in the Warring States Period (475-221 BC). In fact, the water sport could be found in various places in an earlier period. During a race, the boat carries rowers, helmsman, banner bearer and gong and drum beaters. Their division of labor is clearly defined and teamwork is essential. The boat race is preceded by a rite to welcome the dragon out. After it begins, gongs and drums are beaten and the crowds swarm onto the banks to cheer them on. The scene is most thrilling and exciting.

Chinese dragon boat racing enjoys great popularity among the people. When a race is held, participants and spectators are numbered in the thousands or tens of thousands. In order to promote the sport and improve its technical level, in 1984, the State Physical Culture and Sports Commission decided to include dragon boat racing as a formal national competitive sport and to organize the first national "Qu Yuan Cup" dragon boat race in Foshan City, Guangdong Province. The Chinese Dragon Boat Association was established in Yichang City, Hubei Province, on June 6, 1985. The International Dragon Boat Federation was founded in 1995. The first World Dragon Boat Championships were held in Yueyang, Hebei Province, in June of the same year. Apart from the bi-annual event, China has also organized international dragon boat rallies and other events in order to promote the sport more widely in the world.

Kite Flying

Kite flying is a popular traditional sport among the Chinese people. Kites originated in China, with a history going back more than 2000 years. Kites are called the earliest flying

Colorful kites

craft of mankind. Legend has it that a noted carpenter named Lu Ban in the Spring and Autumn Period made a wooden kite and flew it in the wind. Afterwards, people used paper instead of wood to make kites, and they were called "paper kites." In the Han Dynasty and afterwards, people used paper kites to measure distances and convey messages. In the Tang Dynasty, kite flying was introduced into the neighboring countries of Korea and Japan. In the period of the Five Dynasties, bamboo whistles were tied onto the kites. When these kites were flown in the wind, their whistles blew to produce beautiful sounds. As a result, these kites were called "wind kites." By the Song Dynasty, kite flying had gradually become a game providing entertainment for the people.

above: A girl flying her kite in a public square
below: Painting is one of the steps in making kites.

Kite flying was introduced into Europe in the Yuan Dynasty (1279-1368).

Kites are made of fine bamboo slips in a frame covered with paper or crepe and tied with a long string. They rise into the sky through the force of the wind. The techniques of making and flying traditional Chinese kites include "frame-making, paper pasting, painting and flying." The traditional shapes of kites include birds, animals, insects and fish, but in recent years, kites have also been designed in the shape of figures.

Kite flying has become a popular sport and a recreational game in China, enriching

The horse-head zither played at a Nadam Fair in Inner Mongolia

the lives of the people. At the same time, the hard-working Chinese people regard it as an activity which provides exercise, can cure ailment and improve their health.

Nadam Sports Fair

Nadam means "entertainment" or "game" in the Mongolian language. It is a traditional sport of the Mongolian people in China. The five-day annual Nadam Sports Fair which begins on the fourth day of the sixth month on the lunar calendar is a grand gathering of the Mongolian people.

The Nadam Sports Fair includes archery, horse racing and wrestling. In the Yuan Dynasty, the rulers stipulated that all male Mongolians had to acquire the three basic skills of wrestling, horseback riding and shooting arrows. Therefore, the Nadam Fair became a military sports contest. In the Qing Dynasty, Nadam gradually became an officially organized entertainment activity held at the sumu (equivalent to township), with banner (equivalent to country) and league (equivalent to prefecture) levels every six

A fierce battle between two youngsters to seize the headless goat and carry it to the designated spot

months, 12 months or three years. The custom continues even today.

Nadam fairs are divided into three types: large, medium and small. At the large fairs, which last 7-10 days, 512 wrestlers and about 300 fine horses participate. The medium-scale fairs are attended by 256 wrestlers and 100-150 horses, and last 5-7 days. The small ones are attended by 64 or 128 wrestlers, and about 30 to 50 horses, and last 3-5 days. People of all ethnic groups and religions can enter.

When a Nadam Fair is held, people of both sexes and of all age groups, wearing festive clothing, come to the fair by vehicle or horse. They either participate or watch the horse racing, wrestling, archery, dancing and singing activities.

A caravan of horses at the Nadam Fair in Xinjiang

Archery

Archery has a long history among the Mongolian people living in China. After Genghis Khan unified the tribes in Mongolia in the 13th century, the practice of archery developed very quickly. Its horse archery was famous throughout the world. Mu huali, a military advisor, was a famous skilled archer.

In ancient times, Mongolian archers used ox horn bows, rubber band strings and wooden arrows. The shooting distance was 10 to 20 meters. The target for competition was a felt target painted in five different colors, and the target center was movable. It could drop down when it was hit. There was no target in another kind of competition, in which archers shot arrows from dozens of meters away at a ground target, a piled object in the shape of a pagoda. The winner was the archer who hit the target. According to the rules, each archer had four arrows and was required to shoot them all in three rounds. The winner or loser was determined by the number of hits scored. During the competition, the archers wore colorful robes and riding boots.

Folk archer

There are two types of archery competitions: shooting in standing position and shooting in riding position: When shooting in standing position, archers are required to shoot their arrows at the target centers at the same time. If the target center is hit, it automatically falls, and the crowds applaud. Comparatively speaking, shooting on horseback is more popular among the Mongolians. Whenever there is a festival, shooting activities on horseback are held. According to historical records, people shot rabbits in the Liao Dynasty (916-1125), and shot at willows in the Kin Dynasty (1115-1234). In the ensuing Yuan Dynasty, the rulers encouraged the people to learn mounted archery to strengthen the country, as bows and arrows were the main weapons used in warfare.

There are dozens of national traditional sports in China. Apart from those described above, they include horse racing (Mongolian), walking with a pot on the top of the head (Korean), springboard (Korean), kite, yak racing (Tibetan), wrapper throwing (Buyei), elephant tug of war (Tibetan), stick waving (Buyei), pyramid, human dragon (Yao), competing for headless goat (Uygur), swing (Miao), double flying dance (Manchu), climbing knife-ladder (Miao), hopscotch, sandbag throwing (Manchu), flagpole waving (Hui), fiery rope jumping (Yi), figure skipping (Hui), and tossing a colored silk ball (Zhuang).

Horsemanship displayed at a Nadam fair

Development of non-Olympic sports

Non-Olympic sports, an important component of Chinese sports, have grown very fast. The number of non-Olympic sports which are practiced in China has increased from 40 in 1979 to more than 60 at the present time. The technical level of these sports has kept rising, and one-third of them have reached an advanced world level. There have been frequent international exchanges which have enriched the cultural lives of the people in their spare time.

The attraction to the non-Olympic sports in China is very great. As most of the non-Olympic sports are good for fitness, are interesting or can be adventurous or instructive, they are a source of fun for the people.

According to investigations, the top ten non-Olympic sports favored by the Chinese people, in descending order, are: bowling, billiards, golf, weiqi, wushu (including qigong), aerobic exercises, Chinese chess, angling, kite flying and soft tennis. The top ten sports in which the people take an active part are: wushu (including qigong), aerobic exercises, Chinese chess, billiards, weiqi, bridge, bowling,

Increasingly more young people in Chinese cities now enjoying going to the gym

dance sport, soft tennis and angling.

Since the 1950s, non-Olympic sports have played a visibly important role in the great achievements made overall in Chinese sports. According to statistics, between 1979 and 1997, of the 1097 world championships won by Chinese athletes, 74.84 percent were won by athletes in non-Olympic sports.

As China's sports strategy focuses on Olympic sports, its limited funds available for sports have been mostly used on the development of China's major Olympic sports, and the funding needed for the construction of the infrastructure facilities and training of athletes in the non-Olympic sports have obviously been insufficient. At present, the level of participation in sports of the Chinese people is fairly low, as they find it difficult to participate in sports beyond their own financial means. Most of the sports consumption for the present involves the purchase of goods used both for daily life and sports activities and small sports equipment that costs relatively little. Besides, the improvement and popularization of many non-Olympic sports depend largely on the improvement of the equipment, apparatus, venues and other basic conditions. The construction of the infrastructure facilities for non-Olympic sports is still at a fairly low level at present. Improving the basic conditions for non-Olympic sports and intensifying efforts to build more basic facilities in the development of non-Olympic sports has become an urgent task.

Angling

At present, from the perspective of the development of international sports, all countries are enthusiastically giving more publicity to the development of their own national and traditional sports. Every host nation of the Olympic Games and continental games is taking advantage of the host's privilege to add its strong traditional sport to the program, because this is the most effective publicity which can be given to enhance its national dignity, national image and national traditional cultural characteristics. At present, the International Wushu Federation has been recognized by the International Olympic Committee, and this underlines the fact that the Chinese sport of wushu has taken an important step forward on the road to world recognition.

Nationwide fitness campaign

Silk fan dance is a fitness activity favored by Chinese women.

The general standard of health of the populace is of strategic significance to the development of a country. Historically, because of its economic backwardness and especially because of its feudal cultural shackles, the physique of the Chinese people was rather poor compared to other countries. Since the 1950s, the Chinese government has focused on mass sports activities, and the physique of the Chinese people has greatly improved. However, for historical reasons, the management of the mass sports in China has been one of administrative orders under the planned economy for decades. With the reform and opening up to the outside world, since China's market economic system was instituted, the old management over the mass sports is less and less able to meet the actual needs of the people. In the developed countries, sports for the common folks began to develop in the 1970s. In order to meet the fitness needs of their people, many developed countries have one after the other issued documents calling on people to take part in sports and have promulgated various laws to promote the development of sports for the citizens. They have established corresponding organs to ensure the development of the sports for the people, and set up a management structure for this, involving the participation of the government, public organizations and individuals.

The Chinese State Council formally initiated the National Fitness Program in June 1995, in an attempt to change the old mass sports management structure and establish a modern and new national fitness model. A nationwide fitness campaign was launched in 1997. At this point, the social environment and morale for respecting and taking part in sports have initial-

Elderly people enjoying themselves using the fitness equipment installed in community areas

ly taken shape, and the basic framework of a national fitness system with Chinese characteristics has been established. The State Physical Culture and Sports Commission has encouraged all kinds of sports activities to meet the needs of the people for fitness exercises, such as fitness activities for children, young people, farmers, women, workers and the elderly.

The national fitness program consists of three phases. The years from 2001 to 2003

Ping pong is regarded by the Chinese people as their national ball game and is enjoyed by people of all ages.

marked the first phase of consolidation and improvement. The years from 2004 to 2006 marked the second phase of general improvement, and the years 2007 to 2010 mark the phase of all-round development. By 2010, the number of people participating regularly in sports activities throughout China is expected to be around 40 percent of the national population. The physique of the people will be considerably improved, there will be many more venues for sports activities for the people, and efforts will be stepped up to train more public sports instructors who will account for five per thousand of the national population so as to meet the needs of the people for physical exercise.

At the same time, the National Fitness Program has also gained a lot of valuable experience through its bold attempts to reform the mass sports management structure and to set up a mass sports management system and operating mechanism to suit China's market economic system.

A rural sports festival

By 2005, more than 37 percent of the total Chinese population had participated regularly in sports activities. All the communities in the four municipalities directly under the Central Government and the capital cities of the economically developed provinces, 80 percent of the communities in other cities and 25 percent of the rural townships and villages in these municipalities and provinces had set up public sports facilities. In the west and economically less-developed regions, 80 percent of the communities in the provincial capital cities, 60 percent of the communities in other cities and 15 percent of the rural townships had set up public sports facilities. The number of public sports instructors totaled 350,000 throughout the country. More than 70 percent of the neighborhoods in the urban districts, more than 70 percent of the counties and more than 50 percent of the rural townships had set up sports instruction centers. There were around 3,000 sports clubs for juniors established with funding from the sports lotteries.

Construction of stadiums and gymnasiums

China's first sports law was adopted by the Standing Committee of the National People's Congress in 1995. The State Council promulgated the National Fitness Program in the same year. A number of other sports statutes were made public in the subsequent years. The results of an investigation issued by the State Sports Administration show that China's present population involved in sports accounts for 33.9 percent of the total population aged between 7 and 70, and that 60.7 percent of urban residents take part in fitness activities in the various sports clubs. The National Fitness Program intended to improve the physique and level of health of the Chinese people lays its emphasis on the young juniors and children, and encourages the residents to take part in one exercise daily, to learn to do two different exercises, and to have one physical examination every year. In the 15-year program, it is the goal of the government to build a sports and fitness service system for the people. China now has 616,000 outdoor stadiums, gymnasiums, indoor stadiums and sports halls of varying sizes, and most of the sports venues are open to the public. All urban communities, parks, squares, roadside spaces and residential quarters have set up public places with a variety of special equipment and facilities for physical exercising. All communities and rural township neighborhoods in Beijing have installed fitness facilities in line with the requirements of the state. Tianjin has also added indoor and outdoor fitness facilities and venues to the existing facilities on a large scale. China's first large health square which has more than 10,000 square meters was built in Tianjin in 2004.

After China won the privilege to host the 2008 Olympic Games in Beijing, its sports industry has shown its clear market potential, and has tremendous opportunities for its development. This has made the industry more market-oriented. The stadiums and gymnasiums and other facilities have played their growing roles in the sports industry under the market economic conditions. Over the past 50 years and before, China has spent substantial amounts of money to build a large number of stadiums, gymnasiums and other sports facilities, thus providing conditions for the development of China's sports and playing a tremendous role in the fast rise of these sports. Most of China's gold medal winners had been trained in these facilities. Under the socialist market economic conditions today, these stadiums and gymnasiums are still serving the same functions as they did during the period of the planned economy. They are a great contributing factor in the development of sports. They are the stages for sports competitions and performances, the cradles for training world champions, and the important venues for mass sports activities. They are the signs of the development of sports in a city and even in a region and a visible and fixed base for the sports industry. However, they also have inherent shortcomings. They consume a good part of the sports development funds every year, which are used for their maintenance and for expenses related to the working staff. Therefore, making these venues more market oriented is an inevitable tendency. In recent years, the sports facilities have achieved economic results and reduced their use of state funds through various business activities.

Among the existing stadiums and gymnasiums in China at present, those which stand out in terms of their scale of construction and business management approach include:

The 80,000-seat Shanghai Stadium: Built in 1997, it can accommodate 80,000 spectators. It is located southwest of the Tianyao Road Bridge and north of the Zhongshan South Road, and neighbors the Shanghai Swimming Pool. It is a large sports complex based on a new design and covers an area of 190,000 square meters. Its ground surface is circular with a diameter of 300 meters and

Shanghai Stadium with a seating capacity of 80,000 people

the building is shaped like a saddle. The stands are roofed for protection from rain or sunshine. The display halls south of the stadium can be used for various kinds of meetings and discussions, news briefings, and political, economic and cultural activities. It also has comprehensive facilities, including a hotel, an entertainment venue and a shopping mall. China's 8th National Games were held in this complex.

Guangdong Olympic Stadium: Built in 2001, it was the main venue for the 9th Asian Games, and has a seating capacity of 80,000. It is the biggest stadium with the most up-to-date functions in Asia at present, covering a ground area of 300,000 square meters. Its new and unique shape and design have broken away from the traditional

Shandong Provincial Sports Center Stadium

round design concept, and its "silk ribbon" type of roofing design embodies the ideal of free soaring and reflects the pursuit of speed and the longing for the lofty spirit of sports.

Shandong Provincial Sports Center Stadium: Built in 1987, it has a seating capacity of 55,000. It is located at the foot of the Ma'anshan in the southern suburbs of Jinan City. It is 800 meters long from east to west and 280-630 meters wide from north to south on a ground of 33 hectares. The sports complex includes an outdoor stadium, an indoor stadium, an indoor swimming pool, a multi-purpose training hall, a hotel for athletes, outdoor fields and attached facilities. It has four 55-meter-high lighthouses, each weighing 60 tons. They are the highest and heaviest in Asia. It was the main venue for China's 1st National Inter-City Games in 1988, and also accommodated the Asia Cup football tournament in 2004.

Tianjin Olympic Sports Center: As a supporting city for the 2008 Olympic

Tianjin Olympic Sports Center Stadium under construction

Games, Tianjin has begun to build the Olympic Sports Center southwest of Tianjin's urban area. The center consists of a competition area, a multi-purpose area and a dwelling area, including the new outdoor stadium, an indoor stadium and aquatics center, a golf practice field, an international sports exchange center and an Olympic museum.

Beijing Workers' Stadium: This is the eldest member in the family of the Chinese stadiums. It was built in 1959 over an area of 350,000 square meters. Its building area covers 80,000 square meters, and it is one of the ten great buildings completed during that time. The stadium has an oval-shaped concrete frame structure, is 282 meters long from north to south, and 208 meters wide from east to west. It has 24 stands partitioned by railing with a total seating capacity of 71,112. It is now a professional football field meeting the standards prescribed by the FIFA, but can also be used for track and field events and other sports competitions. In the past 48 years, it has witnessed countless sports competitions and various large-scale activities, including the Great Wall Cup Football Invitational Tournament, the Kodak Cup Football Tournament, and the 1st, 2nd, 3rd, 4th, 5th, 7th National Games, the 11th Asian Games, the 6th Far Eastern and South Pacific Games for the Disabled and the "Hongta Cup" Friendly Match with Real Madrid. Apart from the home matches of the Beijing Football Team in the National Division A League, the stadium

Football fans in the Beijing Workers' Stadium

was once the field for the home matches of the Chinese national team.

Wuhan Sports Center Stadium: Built in 2002, it has a seating capacity of 60,000. It is one of the venues for the 2003 Women's World Cup (held in 2007). The stadium (including the football field and the track) covers 22,000 square meters. Both the layout of the football field and the track were built according to the latest standards prescribed by FIFA and IAAF. There are also two standard and closed training fields linked with the stadium by an underground passage.

Hangzhou Yellow Dragon Sports Center Stadium: Built in 2000 near the Yellow Dragon Cave scenic area in Hangzhou, the stadium has a seating capacity for 55,000 spectators. In 2003, it was one of the venues for the Women's Football World Cup Championship. The Yellow Dragon Sports Center is now the largest and most modern sports facility with the greatest number of functions in Zhejiang Province. The stadium, which is its main structure,

A FIFA group inspecting the Wuhan Sports Center Stadium, one of the four venues for the Women's World Cup

stands as one of the landmarks not only of Hangzhou City but also the entire province.

Changsha He Long Stadium: Built in 1987, it can accommodate 55,000 people. It was rebuilt in 2002 to serve as the main stadium for the 5th National Inter-City Games in 2003. Located northwest of the Changshan New Century Sports Cultural Center, the main building has eight stories (partly nine stories) with the lowest altitude of the terraced roof being 28.8 meters and the highest altitude being 33 meters. The whole frame consists of 484 legs. Most of the exterior is decorated with the most popular paneled glass walls in the world. The steel roof has a building space of 45,700 square meters and the steel used weighs 3,552 tons.

Shenyang Wulihe Stadium: The 60,000-seat stadium was first built in 1989 over an area of 30 hectares. It is the main venue for large sports competitions and cultural activities as well as an important place for the development of sports and the growth of the sports industry. It was the main venue for the 2002 World Cup home matches played by the Chinese national team against the other seven teams in Asia to qualify for the final round.

With the 2008 Olympic Games to be held in Beijing, China will add a number of new stadiums and gymnasiums with special characteristics, including the National Stadium or the "Birds' Nest," and the Tianjin Olympic Center Stadium.

The Wulihe Stadium in Shenyang

The sports industry

China's sports industry was established in the 1980s. After 20 years of rapid growth, the framework for the industry has taken shape, and its image as a new growth point of the national economy has been initially formed. Particularly in recent years, sports consumption has kept growing, the sports market has been thriving day by day, and the whole sports industry is becoming one of the new contributing forces that stimulate consumption and increase the domestic demand, and has shown a fairly big growth potential. According to specialists' estimates, the market scale of the Chinese sports industry came close to 80 billion yuan in 1999, and the business income from the sports system (including the income from the sports lotteries) was about 5 billion yuan, about over 60 percent of the total sources of the funding for the sports system.

The successful bid for the 2008 Olympic Games in Bei-

Full-capacity crowd watching a commercial football match played by Real Madrid in China in 2005

jing has provided an opportunity for the development of the sports industry, and at the same time has presented a challenge to the Chinese sports industry.

On the other hand, it is undeniable that sports have become an important industry. This can be seen from the prosperous domestic ball market and the growing number of commercial sports competitions. Turning sports into an industry fits within the reform measures of China's market economic structure, and the inevitable outcome of the rise of China's overall strength and the standard of living of the people as well as the inevitable outcome of the commercial impact of international sports.

Background

For a long time, China practiced a highly unified planned economic system, and society at large and the various sports departments all regarded sports as falling within the framework of public welfare. There was only consumption but no output. The sports developments depended too much on the state. All sports activities were organized, managed and executed by the administrative organs of the state. Emphasis was laid only on more government input, but little attention was paid to self development, and there was even less inherent motivation and vigor for self development.

If sports are to be further developed, if excellent results are to be obtained in the fierce international sports competitions, and if the masses are to be encouraged to participate more in sports and be more excited about sports, this will fundamentally happen through reform.

The practice of relying on administrative orders to manage sports has lost its economic support under the present market economic conditions. It is essential to reform the sports management structure and effect a change in sports not only in the mode of management but also in the structure of business operations so as to increase the ability of the sports to suit the market economic system.

The core of the reform measures in sports is to change the operating mechanism, namely, to completely break away from the old direction of entirely depending upon the government to run sports and to gradually change the welfare orientation to a public orientation and an operational orientation and to establish a mechanism that will lead to a virtuous circle combining state control, public support and self development. The establishment of a virtuous operating mechanism plus the introduction of a corresponding competitive mechanism and bonus mechanism are beneficial to the maximization of the effects of the sports resources, to the flow of sports talents and to the mobilization of the initiatives of sports workers to push forward the further development of sports.

■ The Concept of Making Sports an Industry

The term "sports industry" refers to the industrial sectors which produce, exchange and consume sports products (labor) and provide services to meet the growing needs of the people for sports. From an overall perspective, the sports industry comprises all the economic activities related to sports, such as material sports products (sports clothing, gear, buildings, foods and drinks), sports information products (advertisements, TV broadcasts, press, and news transmissions, etc.), and sports labor (competitions, entertainment, venue leasing, tourism, etc.). Sports were formally included as a tertiary industry in 1985, thereby confirming their industrial character. It can be seen from the components of the sports industry that it covers a wide range of fields and is an industry with a high correlative structure. It is related to many departments of the national economy, i.e., the building industry, manufacturing industry, communications, telecommunications, food, hygiene, information services, clothing and tourism. There is a big potential demand for the sports industry, and it will become one of the most important industrial sectors in the 21st century.

The brisk market of the Chinese football lotteries

Making sports an industry requires an adjustment of the sports structure so that it will have new mechanisms with scope for development and which are full of vigor. It will require the transformation of sports from an institutional department or a public welfare department into a business so that it can provide sports products and service to the society. Its essence is to create a revolution in the ideology and concept of sports, to create innovation in the sports system, and to develop the economic function of sports on the basis of meeting the basic requirements of the market economy. It will also need to conform to the laws of modern sports, and to combine sports with the economy in order to stimulate the demand for sports products (labor) and to exploit the sports market through a series of economic behaviors to accelerate the process of turning sports into an industry so as to instill new vigor into the sustainable development of the national economy.

Development of China's Sports Industry and Its Policies

The sports department is an economic department characterized by a special mode of production. For a considerably long period of time in the past, the relationship between sports and the economy in China was a relationship between sports and finance. Sports were handled by a department which simply dealt with consumption. The financial input of the state into sports affected the development and growth of the sports and their structure, and indirectly determined the influence of the growth of sports on economic growth. As to the proportion and structure of the financial input into sports, overall economic volume is a decisive factor, apart from ideology, concepts and the state policies. The sports industry is built on the basis of socialist economic development, and is in harmony with the socio-economic structure and the level of development. Its management system, operational mechanism, scale and level of development rely on the structural setup and level of economic development of a country. Objectively speaking, sports as an economic department has not yet become an entirely perfect industry within the national economic system in China. The development and growth of the sports industry depend on the cultivation and development of the sports market. Cultivation of the market should start with the factors that affect the formation and development of the market. Only in this way can China make use of the market mechanism to make reasonable allocations and effective use of the sports resources to raise the overall efficiency of sports in the service of society. The per-capita income in China has risen considerably during the present stage of reform, and people have more free time and their demand for sports products (labor) is growing. Given this situation, the only way to make sports an industry is to lose no time in making available sports products which have a good mass foundation and can more easily meet the market demand. Sports should not be a sector that only consumes the resources of the country. The sports industry that integrates hard training, the spirit of going all-out in competition, artistic fitness and the spirit of enhancing the national spirit should become a new growth area of the sustainable development of the national economy.

The process of making sports an industry in China is still in the initial stage at present. The entire sports administrative department is still in a stage of low-level business operation involving the leasing of sports venues and providing paid instruction. Sports as an economic sector has not yet become a mature industrial department so far as its scale, composition and level are concerned. The economic function of sports is still far from being fully developed.

■ Bid for the 27th Olympic Games in 2000
■ Bid for the 29th Olympic Games in 2008
■ The blueprint for the 2008 Olympic Games in Beijing

22:11 hours (Beijing time) on July 13, 2001 was a historical moment in Chinese sports: The right to host the Games of the 29th Olympiad in 2008 was awarded to Beijing, China.

Beijing's
Olympic
Dream

Draft design for China's National Stadium or "Bird's Nest"

Bid for the 27th Olympic Games in 2000

Prelude

After successfully holding the 1990 Asian Games in Beijing, the Chinese people were inspired by the idea of hosting an Olympic Games. On February 13, 1991, the State Physical Culture and Sports Commission, the Ministry of Foreign Affairs, the Ministry of Finance and the Beijing Municipal People's Government jointly submitted to the State Council a report to "Ask for Instructions on Beijing's Application to Bid for the 2000 Olympic Games." Their request received approval. The Beijing Municipal People's Government then formally submitted its request to the Chinese Olympic Committee to host the 27th Olympic Games in Beijing in 2000. The Chinese Olympic Committee held a plenary session. After discussing and reviewing Beijing's application, the session unanimously adopted Beijing's application to be a candidate city for the 27th Olympic Games.

Afterwards, He Zhenliang, president of the Chinese Olympic Committee, sent letters to the leaders and members of the International Olympic Committee, president of the Association of National Olympic Committees, the presidents of the international sports federations and the presidents of the continental Olympic committees, notifying them of the COC's approval of Beijing's application to host the 2000 Olympic Games, and requested their support and cooperation.

On April 1, 1991, the Beijing Olympic Bid Committee held its chairman's working meeting, and announced the formal establishment of the Beijing Candidate Committee for the 2000 Olympic Games. A ceremony was held in the Huiqiao Hotel on May 13th to reveal and establish the board of the Beijing Candidate Committee for the 2000 Olympic Games. At the same time, Beijing set up the Beijing Candidate Committee for the 2000 Olympic Games. Wu Shaozu, minister of the State Physical Culture and Sports Commission, and his group visited the headquarters of the International Olympic Committee, and briefed President Juan Antonio Samaranch about Beijing's bid, and received a supportive reply from President Samaranch and the International Olympic Committee.

Moreover, the Chinese Olympic Committee organized a ceremony to honor Olympic Day on the campus of Peking University. A representative of the university's students read a letter to President Samaranch, expressing the desire of the teachers and students to support Beijing's bid for the 2000 Olympic Games. About 10,000 teachers and students from Peking University, Tsinghua University and the Beijing University of Foreign Studies were present.

Submitting the Application

A delegation from the Beijing Olympic Bid Committee traveled to Lausanne, Switzerland, and submitted its application to the president of the International Olympic Committee in December 1991.

On April 16, 1992, the International Olympic Committee announced that eight cities including Beijing had been chosen as the candidate cities for the 2000 Games. The other cities were Berlin, Brasilia, Istanbul, Manchester, Milan, Sydney and Tashkent. In May, following the submission of the application, a delegation of the Beijing Olympic Bid Committee revisited Lausanne to attend an IOC working meeting of the candidate cities. Their theme slogan was: An Open China Longs for the Olympic Games.

The meeting of the Executive Board of the International Olympic Committee opened in Acapulco, Mexico, on November 6, 1992. The Beijing delegation made an address at the meeting, briefing the IOC members present about the work Beijing had done for the bid. This was the first briefing of the Beijing Olympic Bid Committee to the IOC Executive Committee. In the following year, Wu Zhongyuan and four others of the BOBICO formally submitted Beijing's bid document to President Samaranch at the headquarters of the IOC in Lausanne.

The 12-member IOC Evaluation Commission headed by Gunnar Ericsson, an IOC member, arrived in Beijing on March 6, 1993, to begin its three-day evaluation of Beijing's bid. Premier Li Peng met the IOC group, and assured them that the Chinese government would give full support to Beijing's bid for the 2000 Olympic Games. If Beijing succeeded in its bid, China would have the ability and conditions to success-fully organize the Olympic Games. The Chinese government would give full assurance and support in terms of financial power, material power and human power, and Beijing would greet its friends from all continents with an even more beautiful and more mod-ern city. Afterwards, President Samaranch and Vice President Richard Kevan Gosper and their group undertook another inspection of the work that had been done by Beijing in preparation for the bid.

■Competition

In September 1993, Beijing's Candidate City Delegation, with Vice Premier Li Lanqing as its honorary leader, went to Monte Carlo in Monaco to attend the 101st IOC Session which would decide on the host city for the 2000 Olympic Games, and it made a presentation to the IOC members and the leaders of the international sports organiza-tions that were present.

The secret balloting created great tension. The other candidate cities were Sydney of Australia, Berlin of Germany, Manchester of Britain, and Istanbul of Turkey. Milan of Italy, Brasilia of Brazil and Tashkent of Uzbekistan, which had submitted their bids, withdrew from the competition. There were 88 valid votes cast in the last two rounds. Four rounds of balloting were conducted, but Istanbul and Berlin were eliminated in the first two rounds. In the third round, the votes for Beijing, Sydney, and Manchester were 40, 37 and 11 respectively, and Manchester was thus eliminated. In the first three rounds, the votes for Beijing were 32, 37 and 40, with Beijing leading all along. In the last round, the votes for Sydney and Beijing were 45 and 43. At 2:27 hours in the morn-ing (Beijing time) on September 24, 1993, the eyes of hundreds of millions of people throughout the world were on IOC President Samaranch standing on the platform in the Louis II Gymnasium through the TV screen. At this precise instant, Samaranch uttered the word "Sydney." This meant that the 89 IOC members present at the 101st IOC Ses-sion had chosen Sydney as the host city to organize the 27th Olympic Games in 2000 by secret ballot. Beijing lost the bid. After the announcement was made, members of the

Mr. He Zhenliang briefing retired sports officials on Beijing's first attempt of bidding

Sydney delegation in the gymnasium cheered and jumped for joy. The Chinese living at home and abroad were most disappointed and dejected, but with forced smiles, members of the Beijing delegation politely congratulated the Sydney delegation by waving their hands.

After this first upset, the residents of Beijing became more mature and reasonable. They were waiting for the next chance and their support for the second bid was even stronger. According to the world-known Gallup (China) Ltd., 94.9 percent of Beijing's residents supported the bid, while the independent sampling conducted by a European company entrusted by the IOC to do the sampling in the five candidate cities showed that Beijing had the support of 96 percent of its residents for the bid.

Bid for the 29th Olympic Games in 2008 |

When it comes to the Olympic Games, participation is of great importance. The process of bidding for the Olympic Games was one involving participation, promoting China's construction and development, stimulating the national morale and enhancing national cohesiveness. Viewed from this perspective, a bid is of great significance whether it is successful or not.

The Second Bid

On November 25, 1998, Beijing formally submitted its application to host the 2008 Olympic Games to the Chinese Olympic Committee, and received its approval.

On April 7, 1999, Liu Qi, mayor of Beijing, and Wu Shaozu, former president of the Chinese Olympic Committee, formally submitted Beijing's report on the bid for the 2008 Olympic Games to Samaranch, President of the IOC in Lausanne. The Chinese departments involved formed the Beijing Bid Commit-

A press conference in Beijing on bidding for the Olympic Games of 2008

tee for the 2008 Olympic Games, with its headquarters located in the Xinqiao Hotel. This marked the formal start of the bidding process. Soon afterwards, the BOBICO decided on its logo and slogan, and also opened its website. The logo was jointly designed by three artists named Chen Shaohua, Han Meilin and Jin Daiqiang. It is a five-pointed star formed by the five interlaced Olympic rings, and at the same time it represents the image of the traditional folk art "Chinese knot," symbolizing the unity and development of the five continents of the world. The five-pointed star is the symbol of the nation and the figure of a taiji boxer, displaying the quintessence of the traditional Chinese sports culture.

■Six Reasons for the Bid

On February 1, 2000, Liu Qi, president of the BOBICO, expounded on China's six reasons for the bid:

First, as the most populous country in the world, China should make its contribution to developing the Olympic Movement and promoting world peace.

Second, it is the strong desire of the people of Beijing and of the whole country to

Beijing's residents showing their support to the Olympic bid

host the Olympic Games, and it has received powerful support from the Chinese government.

Third, in the more than 20 years since it started the process of reform and opening to the outside world, China has made achievements that have captured the attention of the world in all spheres including its society, economy and culture.

Fourth, organization of the Olympic Games can accelerate environmental protection and promote economic development. It is a beneficial opportunity for Beijing in its march towards the new millennium.

Fifth, hosting the Olympic Games will promote the development of Chinese sports and further enhance the universality of the Olympic Movement.

Sixth, the bid is beneficial to the development of Beijing as a modern international metropolis. By taking advantage of the bid, we can display to the whole world our an-

The "New Beijing, Great Olympics" sculpture on Wangfujing Street attracts tourists from all parts of the world.

cient and profound cultural traditions, our tolerance and broadmindedness, our public virtues of modesty and politeness, and our pioneering spirit of hard work.

■The Second Application

On February 2, 2000, the International Olympic Committee announced that ten cities had submitted applications to the IOC to bid for the 2008 Olympic Summer Games by the deadline of February 1. They were Beijing of China, Bangkok of Thailand, Istanbul of Turkey, Kuala Lumpur of Malaysia, Havana of Cuba, Cairo of Egypt, Osaka of Japan, Paris of France, Seville of Spain and Toronto of Canada. Soon afterwards, Liu Jingmin, executive vice president of the Beijing Olympic Bid Committee, led a group to attend a joint meeting of the applicant cities for the 2008 Olympic Games, and each of the applicant cities was asked 22 questions from six categories by the IOC. The IOC Executive Committee would choose the candidate cities on the basis of their "answers." The meeting announced a new bid procedure and the candidate cities were informed of three things that would not be permitted: The IOC members were not permitted to visit the candidate cities, the candidate cities were not permitted to visit the IOC members, and the candidate cities were not permitted to give gifts.

On June 19, 2000, Wang Wei, then secretary-general of the BOBICO, sent 50 copies of Beijing's application document to the IOC in Lausanne. As required by the IOC, the application document answered the 22 questions in all six categories. The IOC announced in Lausanne that the ten applicant cities had all submitted their application documents to the IOC by the deadline.

■The Final Phase

On July 25, 2000, Beijing formally chose Qingdao as the candidate city for the yachting events of the Beijing Olympic Games in 2008.

At 19:39 hours on August 28, 2000, Beijing became one of the candidate cities for 29th Olympic Games in 2008. The other candidate cities were: Istanbul, Osaka, Paris and Toronto. This marked the beginning of the final phase of the process involved in the bidding for the 2008 Olympic Games.

On September 9, 2008, the Beijing Olympic Bid Committee received a faxed notice from IOC Director General Francoise Carrard to the effect that that the logo with the English words "Candidate City" and the IOC five-ring emblem had been approved by the IOC.

On September 25, 2000, the IOC called a meeting of the five chosen candidate cities for the 2008 Olympic Games in Sydney, and announced to the five candidate cities the dates for the inspections by the IOC Evaluation Commission. Beijing would be the first city to be inspected by the Commission from February 20 through 25, 2001. On October 27, 2000, the five candidate cities, i.e., Osaka, Paris, Toronto, Beijing and Istanbul, made 20-minute presentations in Monte Carlo as required by the IOC.

On November 3, Liu Qi, mayor of Beijing and president of the BOBICO, engaged 11 celebrities in Hong Kong and Macao, including Henry Fok and Li Kasheng, as advisors to the BOBICO in Hong Kong on behalf of the Beijing Bid Committee for the 2008 Olympic Games.

On December 13, 2000, the BOBICO delegation made a presentation on its work to the IOC Executive Committee at the IOC headquarters in Lausanne, and stated that Beijing had the confidence, conditions and ability to successfully host the 2008 Olympic Games, and that the Chinese Olympic Committee would give full support to Beijing in its bid for the Games. Wang Wei, BOBICO secretary-general, explained to the IOC Executive Committee Beijing's concept of "Green Olympics, Scientific Olympics and People's Olympics," and its Olympic venue plan.

On December 25, 2000, the Beijing Bid Committee for the 2008 Olympic Games received certificates of authentication from all 28 international Olympic summer sports federations. It engaged Deng Yaping, Gong Li, Yang Lan and Sang Lan as image ambassadresses for Beijing's Olympic bid. Earlier, it had engaged Jackie Chan as an image ambassador for the bid.

■Evaluation

At 10:00 in the morning on January 17, 2001, Secretary-general Wang Wei and his five-member group submitted Beijing's bid documents for the 2008 Olympic Games to the IOC in Lausanne. The IOC announced that it had received the bid documents from all five candidate cities.

On February 2, 2001, the sampling conducted by the Gallup (China) Consultancy Co. Ltd. revealed that 94.9 percent of Beijing's residents supported Beijing's bid. At the same time, 94 percent of Beijing's residents expressed their wish to be volunteers for the Games. The poll was taken by Gallup independently in November 2000. Its sampling results were included in Beijing's bid document.

In February 2001, members of the IOC Evaluation Commission arrived in Beijing. The commission gave a press conference after its evaluation and spoke positively of Beijing's bid. After receiving the report of the IOC Evaluation Commission in Lausanne, the Beijing Olympic Bid Committee was very excited although it was what it had expected.

■Presentation

The 112th IOC Session opened in the Bolshoi Theater in Moscow with the playing of the Russian national anthem and the Olympic Hymn on the evening of July 12, 2001. The following day in Moscow was sunny with a gentle breeze. The meeting to decide on the host city for the 2008 Olympic Games was held in the famous International Trade Center in the downtown core of the city. At noon, the delegations of the five candidate cities entered the meeting hall one after the other. At 13 hours, the meeting was formally started. At 13:30, Samaranch, who presided over the meeting, asked the Osaka delegation to start its presentation.

Members of the Osaka delegation, all in traditional national costumes, first showed a short film introducing Japan's customs and scenery. Geishas in silk robes sang and danced, flags of carp fluttered in the breeze, cranes flew into the distance in the setting sun, and Mount Fuji was sparklingly bright.... The film was in rich color and had a great impact on the audience. At the very beginning of the presentation, a 14-year-old girl named Misayan played the Olympic Hymn on her violin to express her yearning for the Olympic Games. Osaka's "Sports Paradise on the Sea" was undoubtedly fascinating. Its mayor Takafumi Isomura said that the city planned to build two artificial islands in its bay, and they

Members of the Beijing Olympic Bid Committee delegation in Moscow on July 13, 2001

would be named Olympic Islands.

At 14:45, the Paris delegation began its presentation. The golden rays of sunlight shone over the blue Seine, the summer monsoon lightly touched the exquisite sculptures, the Eiffel Tower, the Arch of Triumph, the Louvre, the Notre-Dame de Paris, and the Pompidou Center.... The film about Paris was a perfect miniature art film. It enticed the audience to follow a blonde beauty to feel the shock of the beauty of the "Capital of Arts" in all dimensions. It also blended the spots completely into the daily life of Paris through the presence of an old man and a child.

The Toronto delegation was very bold. Amidst the beating of hand drums with singing by two aboriginals, an Indian tribal chief from Toronto introduced the members of the delegation. The mayor of Toronto laid emphasis on the mixture of the multiple cultures and multiple nationalities, saying that everything in the Olympic Games to be held in Toronto would center on the athletes. A girl sang an appealing song with a lively rhythm, and many IOC members responded with applause and beat in rhythm.

At 19 hours sharp, the Beijing delegation entered the conference hall. It was quiet inside, but the confidence revealed in the eyes of the members of the delegation made people hear clearly one voice shouting: "Beijing, yes, you are coming again!"

Beijing's presentation started with Chinese IOC member He Zhenliang introducing the members of the Beijing delegation in fluent French. Li Lanqing, member of the Standing Committee of the Central Committee of the Chinese Communist Party and vice

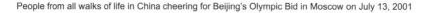

People from all walks of life in China cheering for Beijing's Olympic Bid in Moscow on July 13, 2001

premier of the State Council, made a presentation on behalf of the Chinese government. He stressed that the Chinese government would firmly support the stand of Beijing in bidding for the 2008 Olympic Games, and that the Chinese government would respect and appreciate the evaluation of the IOC Evaluation Commission. In the past half century, the Chinese people had considerably raised their level of health thanks to the nationwide fitness campaign as well as other factors. China had become one of the countries in the world with the fastest rate of economic growth. He promised that if the Olympic Games closed with a surplus, China would establish an Olympic Friendship Foundation to help other developing counties to develop their sports. If there were a deficit, the Chinese government would cover it.

Mr. He Zhenliang making a presentation

Yuan Weimin, president of the Chinese Olympic Committee; Liu Qi, mayor of Beijing; and Lou Dapeng, sports director of the Beijing Olympic Bid Committee; Deng Yaping and Yang Lan, image ambassadresses for Beijing's Olympic bid, and Yang Ling, Olympic shooting champion in Sydney, all in turn made their presentations. Their faces were full of smiles and their words expressed their deep feelings. Their presentations were followed by a short film which showed the winding Great Wall on the top of the mountains, Chinese kung fu, the traditional gongs and drums ... the flowing red, yellow and black colors represented the colors of the Chinese land, the colors of the Chinese sons and daughters. The ancient land of China and its 5,000-year historical accumulation emerged like a torrential river rushing down into the sea. This moment really belonged to China!

After the Beijing delegation finished their presentations in ten minutes, eight IOC members asked 11 questions. It took the delegation nearly 20 minutes to answer these questions. All the questions were very realistic. They covered matters such as pollution control, competition venues, language communication issues, anti-doping, transportation and distribution of the surplus.

The last candidate city to make a presentation was Istanbul.

■Instant Moment

A mock ballot took place at 21:50 hours. The IOC members began the formal balloting at 22 hours to elect the host city for the 2008 Olympic Summer Games. The first round of votes ended in five minutes. Samaranch announced the result of the first round of votes — Osaka was out. The IOC quickly started the second round of voting. After another five long minutes of waiting, an IOC member received a sheet of paper with

After Samaranch's announcement, people in China poured out onto the streets to celebrate the victory.

the count of the votes. He smiled, put the paper into an envelope and closed it carefully. This indicated that the final decision had been made. He stood up, walked over to Samaranch, and gave the letter to him. After a brief exchange of words, Samaranch took the letter and walked to the podium. His expression revealed no hint of which city had won the great honor.

Samaranch opened the letter, took out the sheet, and announced solemnly: "The winner of the 2008 Olympic Games is — Beijing."

The conference hall was seething with cheers and applause. Members of the Chinese delegation were all overjoyed. They hugged each other and savored their joy to their hearts' content.

According to the rules, a candidate city must obtain 52 votes to win the right to host the 2008 Olympic Games. In the first round, Beijing received 44 votes, Toronto 20 votes, Istanbul 17 votes, Paris 15 votes and Osaka 6 votes. In the second round, Beijing received 56 votes, Toronto 22 votes, Paris 18 votes and Istanbul 9 votes. At 22:10 hours on July 13, 2001, Beijing was awarded the right to host the 29th Olympic Games in 2008.

We must never become dizzy with success nor lose heart because of failure. This is the magnanimity and manner which the Chinese people should adopt. The day is no longer far away when the Olympic five-ring flag flies high and the Olympic flame burns in this Eastern country with one-fifth of the world's population, a land of 9.6 million square kilometers and 5,000 years of civilization.

The blueprint for the 2008 Olympic Games in Beijing |

In 2006, when the interval between Olympic Games was nearly at its halfway mark, China published the Olympic slogans, announced the Olympic mascot and the Olympic emblem.

■Olympic Venue Construction

The construction of Olympic venues has always been the focus of attention. The designs of all Olympic venues have won admiration from countless visitors.

The heart of the 2008 Olympic Games — the Olympic Green, contains 44 percent of the Olympic competition venues and most of the facilities in the service of the Olympic Games. The Olympic Green is located at the northern end of the extension of Beijing's central line. It has 14 competition venues, and each of these venues is a five-minute bus drive from the Olympic Village. It also includes the Press Village, the Main Press Center, the International Broadcasting Center, a museum and an exhibition hall. These venues will provide services to the spectators, athletes and interme-

diaries. The "Bird's Nest" or the National Stadium with its very original architectural style, which emerged from among the international bids, has been regarded by experts as a sports building exhibiting the highest standards of international architecture in the early 21st century. Its construction will add modern vigor to the ancient city of Beijing, and will turn the guiding thought of "New Beijing, Great Olympics" into a reality. The National Aquatics Center, otherwise called the "Water Cube," stands on the other side of

The "Bird's Nest," the main stadium for the 2008 Olympic Games, under construction

The Water Cube — the aquatics center for the 2008 Olympic Games

a road and opposite to the National Stadium. It is the biggest in size, most complicated in structure and most comprehensive in technology in the world. Its exterior is the ETFE film looking like water bubbles. The design secret behind it gives play to the wild fanciful thoughts of the visitors.

As to the venues, the Chinese Olympic Committee does not seek novelty. Its main considerations are: one, to be able to increase the post-Olympic frequency of usage of the venues; two, to make full use of the existing sports facilities and raise the frequency of usage of the sports facilities in Beijing; three, to use as many temporary facilities as possible and to build fewer new venues so as to avoid having buildings which subsequently stand idle. There will be innovations, as well as careful consideration and reasonable arrangements. The optimal plan for the construction of Olympic venues in Beijing is in full compliance with the IOC's weight-reducing idea and the popularization of knowledge about the Olympics. Moreover, the selected sites for field hockey, baseball, softball, tennis and beach volleyball have been accepted by the International Olympic Committee and the International Sports Federations which are involved.

■Dancing Beijing — the Emblem of the Olympic Games in 2008

When the yellow satin cover was taken away and the padauk box was opened, a glistening Chinese seal appeared and the emblem of the 29th Olympic Games in 2008 was revealed from behind the mystical veil. The emblem treasure, named the "Chinese

Seal, Dancing Beijing," dipped in red ink paste, was solemnly stamped onto a piece of Xuan paper. From that moment on, Dancing Beijing has opened its two arms to welcome friends from all continents and has joined the world in dancing.

The emblem consists of the seal form, the words "Beijing 2008" and the Olympic rings. The seal form looks like the Chinese character for "jing," meaning capital city, and a dancing figure, elegant and graceful, with athletic features. It adopts the Chinese traditional artistic forms of seal, calligraphy and ancient characters carved on tortoise shells and skillfully integrates the Chinese spirit, charm and culture to symbolize the image of China opening to the outside world, full of vigor and with a promising future.

With the seal stamped, the 1.3 billion Chinese have, with their most solemn and sacred etiquette, made their serious promise to the world to organize Beijing Olympics 2008 into the most outstanding Olympic Games event in history. Moreover, all the dimensions of the Olympic emblem have their special symbolism: the side is 11.2 centimeters long, representing the period of 112 years from 1896 to 2008 which the Modern Olympic Games have covered; the seal body is 2.9 centimeters high, implying the 29th Olympiad; and the top of the seal is 9.6 centimeters high, symbolizing China's land area of

The emblem of the Beijing Olympic Games in 2008

A franchise shop selling souvenirs of the 2008 Olympic Games

9.6 million square kilometers. The total height of the seal is 13 centimeters, implying that the 1.3 billion Chinese people are longing for the Olympic Games. The use of a piece of green and white jade for making the emblem also contains four messages: take benevolence from jade, and be kind and generous to others to represent the Olympic spirit of magnanimity; take wisdom from jade and be determined to go forward to represent the Olympic spirit of innovation and advancement; take courage from jade and be dauntless in representing the Olympic spirit of "citius, altius, fortius" (faster, higher and stronger); and take cleanliness from jade and be free of even a speck of dust to represent the Olympic spirit of loftiness and purity.

The two emblem seals have been carved with meticulous care from the same jade produced in Hotan in Xinjiang, and their exterior design is the best chosen from among the 1,985 works of art collected from inside and outside of China. One of them will be kept in the Chinese Museum, and the other will be sent to the Olympic Museum in Lausanne, Switzerland, for permanent safekeeping as historical witness to the active participation of 1.3 billion Chinese people in the Olympic Movement.

■The Mascots of the 2008 Olympic Games — Welcome to Beijing

Beibei is the Fish, Jingjing is the Panda, Huanhuan is the Olympic Flame, Yingying is the Tibetan Antelope and Nini is the Swallow.

For a long, long time, China has had the tradition of spreading wishes and blessings through signs and symbols. Each of the mascots for the Beijing Olympic Games symbolizes a different blessing: Prosperity, happiness, passion, health and good luck. Carrying the profound friendship of the Chinese people, they will send their blessings to all corners of the world and invite the athletes and the people of all countries to meet in Beijing to celebrate the grand 2008 Olympic festival. The Beijing mascots have been made to resemble five little children, and therefore have even deeper meanings. "Beibei,"

"Jingjing," "Huanhuan," "Yingying," and "Nini," and each of these Fuwa has a rhyming two-syllable name — a traditional way of expressing affection for children in China. When the names of the five Fuwa are put together, they say "Bei Jing Huan Ying Ni" (Welcome to Beijing). Moreover, the five children also symbolize sports and blessings.

Beibei carries the message of prosperity. Its head pattern is a pattern of fish in China's Neolithic Age. In traditional Chinese culture and arts, "fish" and "water" patterns are symbols of prosperity and harvest. People use the fable of the "carp leaping over the

Fuwa — mascots for Beijing's Olympic Games

dragon's gate" to imply success in one's career and the fulfillment of one's dreams. "Fish" also implies the meaning of "auspicious happiness in superabundance" and "a surplus year after year." Beibei is sweet and pure. She is a top athlete, and is radiant together with the Olympic blue ring.

Jingjing is a lovely panda. He brings joy and happiness to people wherever he goes. As China's national treasure, the panda has been an animal beloved by all the people of the world. Jinjing symbolizes the harmonious relationship between man and nature. The lotus design on his headdress is based on the porcelain paintings in the Song Dynasty. He is honest and optimistic, and is full of strength. He represents the Olympic black ring.

The mascots were announced on November 11, 2005.

Huanhuan is the eldest brother of the five. He is a baby of fire, symbolizing the Olympic flame. He is the incarnation of the passion of sport and carries the Olympic message of "faster, higher and stronger." Wherever he goes, he brings Beijing's warmth to the world. The fire design on his head is derived from flames found in the Dunhuang Grottoes. He is open and outgoing. He excels in all ball games and symbolizes the Olympic red ring.

Yingying symbolizes a fast and agile Tibetan antelope. He comes from the vast land in China's western part and carries the beautiful blessing of good health to all parts of the world. He is a unique and protected species of animal found on the Qinghai-Tibet Plateau, and a symbol of the Green Olympics. The design of his headdress is drawn from the decorative styles on the west regions of the Qinghai-Tibetan Plateau and Xinjiang. He is agile and quick as a track athlete and represents the Olympic yellow ring.

Nini is a flying swallow in the sky. Swallow is pronounced "yan" in Chinese, and Yanjing is what Beijing was called as an ancient capital city. Nini brings spring and happiness to the people, and spreads the beautiful blessing of "Good blessing to you" wherever she flies past. Innocent, cheerful and agile, she will compete in the gymnastics events. She represents the Olympic green ring.

■The Same Wish — Slogan for the 2008 Olympic Games

China is a country with strong aspirations. Its people are very reserved. However, once their enthusiasm is aroused they will pursue their dreams together in a most heartfelt manner.

The new slogan for the 2008 Olympic Games in Beijing is "One World, One Dream." "One World" means that the Olympic Movement is one family, and the people are united in their similar experiences at the Olympic Games. Although they differ from individual to individual, their journey through life and their longing for friendship and peace are similar. We live together during this grand Olympic festival through fair competition under the Olympic flag irrespective of our political or religious beliefs, economic system or cultural origin. We constitute a fair and equal world. "One dream" means that we not only live together peacefully and seek development together in this world, but pursue a "still better world." The "grand festival" during the Olympic Games will bring joy and happiness to the whole world, and it is the common goal of all members of the Olympic family to sustain such joy.

"One World, One Dream" is a slogan expressing harmony, common experience and world unity. It reflects the goal of the Olympic Movement to unite the whole world through sports, and expresses the wish of the Chinese people to embrace the world through friendship. It portrays the common experience that the Olympic Games brings to the people, and conveys the common voice of the people and their longing for a better future, and gives expression to the values of unity, harmony, sharing and dreaming.

The pictograms of Beijing 2008

Appendix ⌒

Appendix I Major International Sports Events Held in China

The 2008 Olympic Games will be held on Chinese territory after the efforts of generations of Chinese people. Prior to the Olympic Games, China had organized many other international sporting events, which to a certain extent laid the foundation for the successful bid in 2001, and provided valuable experience in organizing the 2008 Olympic Games. These events served as prequels and preparations for the 2008 Olympic Games.

■The 11th Asian Games in 1990

The 11th Asian Games, lasting for 16 days, were held in Beijing from September 22 through October 7, 1990. This was the first Asian Games China had ever hosted. It was attended by 6,122 athletes from 37 countries and regions in Asia (except for Iraq and Jordan).

Holding aloft the banner of "unity, friendship and progress" and carrying forward the Olympic spirit of "citius, altius, fortius," the Asian

Games represented a bright new chapter in promoting the development of sports in Asia and the world, and laid a solid foundation for China's bid for the Olympic Games. The successful organization of the Asian Games in Beijing was a new contribution made by the Chinese people to the Olympic Games held in Asia. The games displayed the wisdom and talent of the Asian people and highlighted the new level of the rise of Asian sports.

The Chinese delegation won the gold medals with a sweeping force. They took 183 gold medals, 107 silver medals and 51 bronze medals, bringing the total medal count to 341. The Chinese delegation captured more than half of all the gold medals at the 11th Asian Games.

■The 21st World University Students Games

The 21st World University Students Games opened in Beijing on August 21, 2001. A total of 3,939 athletes, 2,751 coaches and officials, as well as 2,243 journalists were present.

The Athletes' Apartments during the 21st World University Students Games

The Chinese delegation made history at the Games by taking 54 gold medals, 25 silver medals and 24 bronze medals to top the gold medal tally at a world games for the first time. China made a clean sweep of the gold medals in diving and table tennis.

■Beijing International Marathon Races

The First Beijing International Marathon Race took place on September 27, 1981. The race, which has taken place once a year since that time, has now become a traditional international event with considerable influence. It attracts more than 10,000 athletes every year, thus becoming one of the major marathon races in the world. The best time recorded so far is 2 hours 7 minutes and 35 seconds. Chinese runner Hu Gangjun won the 1993 race in 2 hours 9 minutes and 18 seconds, also the best time for Chinese marathoners.

Other international marathon races have been held in the Chinese cities of Shanghai,

The Beijing International Marathon Race

Dalian, Jinan, Qingdao and Xiamen.

■ The 9th Sudirman Cup Badminton

The 9th Sudirman Cup Badminton was held in Beijing from May 10 through 15, 2005. More than 500 top players from 42 countries competed in the Cup matches, which marked the highest level team badminton event. This was one of the major pre-Olympic sports events organized in Beijing.

■ Other Major Sports Events Held in China

The 43rd World Table Tennis Championships were held in Tianjin in 1995. The Chinese team made a clean sweep of the gold medals in the seven-event tournament.

The Thomas Cup and Uber Cup Badminton Championships were held in Guangzhou in 2002.

The Asian Cup Football Tournament was held in four Chinese cities, with the finals played in Beijing in 2004. A total of 41 teams played in the preliminaries.

The 1st International Triathlon was held in the Shisanling Reservoir area in Changping District, Beijing, on September 12, 2004.

In May 2005, Shanghai hosted the 48th World Table Tennis Championships. The events on the program were men's and women's singles, men's and women's doubles, and mixed doubles.

Beijing hosted the Stankovic Intercontinental Basketball Championships in 2005. This event is known as the "Small World Cup Basketball."

China 1st IBA World Professional Boxing Championships was held in the Capital Gymnasium in Beijing on August 20, 2005.

The Diving Competition of the 7th Asian Swimming Championships was held at the Diving Center in Chenzhou, Hunan, on September 11, 2005.

Appendix II China's Sports Organizations
(in Chinese and English)

国家体育总局	State Sport Administration
中华全国体育总会	All-China Sports Federation
中国奥林匹克委员会	Chinese Olympic Committee
中国田径协会	Chinese Athletics Association
中国足球协会	Chinese Football Association
中国篮球协会	Chinese Basketball Association
中国排球协会	Chinese Volleyball Association
中国游泳协会	Chinese Swimming Association
中国网球协会	Chinese Tennis Association
中国桥牌协会	Chinese Bridge Association
中国武术协会	Chinese Wushu Association
中国乒乓球协会	Chinese Table Tennis Association
中国羽毛球协会	Chinese Badminton Association
中国滑冰协会	Chinese Skating Association
中国自行车协会	Chinese Cycling Association
中国健美操协会	Chinese Aerobics Association
中国柔道协会	Chinese Judo Association
中国拳击协会	Chinese Boxing Association
体育设施标准管理办公室	Sports Facilities Standard Authority

北京奥运大厦

Beijing 2002

The Beijing Olympic Mansion

Roller skating, a popular sport among children

Mongolian-style wrestling, a traditional sport of the Mongolian ethnic people

The winners are the stronger ones.

图书在版编目（CIP）数据

中国体育: 光荣与梦想: 英文/张永恒编著.

—北京: 外文出版社, 2008（全景中国）

ISBN 978-7-119-05390-5

I. 中... II. 张... III. 体育事业—概况—中国—英文 IV. G812

中国版本图书馆CIP数据核字（2008）第078322号

全景中国—中国体育: 光荣与梦想

主　　编：张永恒
图片提供：李石营　韩建明　CFP（排名不分先后）

中文审定：萧师铃
英文翻译：章挺权　周晓刚
英文审定：Solange Silverberg　黄友义
责任编辑：刘芳念
封面设计：蔡　荣
印刷监制：冯　浩

© 2008 外文出版社
出版发行：
外文出版社（中国北京百万庄大街24号）
邮政编码 100037　http://www.flp.com.cn
印　　制：
北京外文印刷厂

中国国际图书贸易总公司发行（中国北京车公庄西路35号）
北京邮政信箱第399号　邮政编码 100044

开本: 980mm×710mm 1/16（平装）　印张:12.25
2008年6月第1版第1次印刷
(英)
ISBN 978-7-119-05390-5
09800
85-E-643P